Nadine is looking at me almost pityingly. 'You'll see, Ellie,' she says. 'When you get a proper boy-friend of your own.'

That's it.

My mouth opens and starts talking. 'Oh don't worry, I've *got* a boyfriend,' I say, before I can stop myself.

Nadine stares at me.

Magda stares at me.

It's like I've nipped out around my glasses and I'm staring at me too.

What have I just said???

What am I doing?

How come I started this?

But I can't stop now . . .

The first book in Jacqueline Wilson's bestselling trilogy for teenage readers.

girls in ♥ love

GIRLS IN LOVE
A CORGI BOOK : 0 552 55131 7

First published in Great Britain by Doubleday

PRINTING HISTORY
Doubleday edition published 1997
Corgi edition published 1998
This edition published 2003

3 5 7 9 10 8 6 4

Copyright © Jacqueline Wilson, 1997
Illustrations copyright © Nick Sharratt, 1997

The right of Jacqueline Wilson to be identified as the author of this work has
been asserted in accordance with the Copyright Designs and Patents Act 1988

Set in Bembo
by Phoenix Typesetting, Ilkley, West Yorkshire.

Corgi Books are published by Random House Children's Books,
61–63 Uxbridge Road, London W5 5SA,
a division of The Random House Group Ltd,
in Australia by Random House Australia (Pty) Ltd,
20 Alfred Street, Milsons Point, Sydney, NSW 2061, Australia,
in New Zealand by Random House New Zealand Ltd,
18 Poland Road, Glenfield, Auckland 10, New Zealand
and in South Africa by Random House (Pty) Ltd,
Endulini, 5a Jubilee Road, Parktown 2193, South Africa.

Printed and bound in Great Britain by
Cox & Wyman Ltd, Reading, Berkshire.

Jacqueline Wilson

girls in ♥ love

CORGI BOOKS

Nine Dedications!

1. Stephanie Dummler and Year Nine Venus (1995), Coombe Girls School.
2. Becky Heather and Year Nine Chestnut and Beech (1995), The Green School for Girls.
3. Jane Ingles and the pupils of Hillside School.
4. Claire Drury and the pupils of Failsworth School – especially Jackelyn and Rachel.
5. Sarah Greenacre and the pupils of the Stoke High School.
6. De Reading and the pupils of St Benedict School.
7. Angela Derby.
8. Becki Hillman.
9. To all the other schools who made me so welcome in 1995 and 1996.

Nine Major Resolutions

1. Stay best friends with Magda and Nadine.

2. Draw every day - and come top in Art. **1st**

3. Try not to come bottom in all other subjects!

4. Go on a diet and STICK to it.
   (No more Magnum ice-creams, sob sob.)

5. Do something with my hair. Anything. Grow it.
   Or cut it right off. Dye it ???

6. Get some sort of paid work the minute I'm fourteen
   so I can...

7. Buy some decent clothes.

8. Go clubbing. •Seventh Heaven•

9. **GET A BOYFRIEND!**

One Girl

The first day back at school. I'm walking because I missed the bus. *Not* a good start. Year Nine. I wonder what it'll be like.

Number nine, number nine, number nine . . .

It's on that classic Beatles White album, the crazy mixed-up bit at the end. I've always felt close to John Lennon even though he died before I was born. I like him because he did all those crazy little drawings and he wore granny glasses and he was funny and he always just did his own thing. I do crazy little drawings and I wear granny glasses and my friends think I'm funny. I don't get the opportunity to do my own thing though.

It's half past eight. If I was doing my own thing right now I'd be back in bed, curled up, fast asleep. John Lennon had lie-ins, didn't he, when he and

Yoko stayed in bed all day. They even gave inter-
views to journalists in bed. Cool.

So, if I could do my own thing I'd sleep till
midday. Then breakfast. Hot chocolate and dough-
nuts. I'll listen to music and fool around in my
sketchbook. Maybe watch a video. Then I'll eat
again. I'll send out for a pizza. Though maybe I
should stick to salads. I guess it would be easy to put
on weight lying around in bed all day. I don't want
to end up looking like a beached whale.

I'll have a green salad. And green grapes. And
what's a green drink? There's that liqueur I sipped
round at Magda's, crème de menthe. I can't say I was
that thrilled. It was a bit like drinking toothpaste.
Forget the drink.

I'll phone Magda though, and Nadine, and we'll
have a long natter. And then . . .

Well, it'll be the evening now, so I'll have a bath
and wash my hair and change into . . . What should
I wear in bed? Not my own teddy-bear nightie.
Much too babyish. But I don't fancy one of those
slinky satin numbers. I know, I'll wear a long white
gown with embroidered roses all colours of the
rainbow, and I'll put a big flash ring on every finger
and lie flat in my bed like Frida Kahlo. She's another
one of my heroes, this amazing South American
artist with extraordinary eyebrows and earrings and
flowers in her hair.

OK, there I am, back in bed and looking
beautiful. Then I hear the door opening. Footsteps.
It's my boyfriend coming to see me . . .

The only trouble is I haven't *got* a boyfriend.

Well, I haven't got a Frida Kahlo outfit or a bedside phone or my own television and video and my bed sags because my little brother Eggs uses it as a trampoline whenever I'm not around. I could put up with all these deprivations. I'd just like a boyfriend. Please.

Just as I'm thinking this a beautiful blond boy with big brown eyes comes sauntering round a car parked partly on the pavement. He steps to one side to get out of my way, only I've stepped the same way. He steps to the other side. So do I! We look like we're doing a crazy kind of two-step.

'Oh. Whoops. Sorry!' I stammer. I feel my face flooding scarlet.

He stays cool, one eyebrow slightly raised. He doesn't say anything but he smiles at me.

He smiles at me!

Then he walks neatly past while I dither, still in a daze.

I look back over my shoulder. He's looking back at me. He really is. Maybe . . . maybe he likes me. No, that's mad. Why should this really incredible guy who must be at least eighteen think anything of a stupid schoolgirl who can't even walk past him properly?

He's not looking up. He's looking down. He's looking at my legs! Oh, God, maybe my skirt really *is* too short. I turned it up myself last night. Anna said she'd shorten it for me, but I knew she'd only turn it up a centimetre or so. I wanted my skirt really short. Only I'm not that great at sewing. The hem went a bit bunchy. When I tried the skirt back on there suddenly seemed a very large amount of chubby pink leg on show.

Anna didn't say anything but I knew what she was thinking.

Dad was more direct: 'For God's sake, Ellie, that skirt barely covers your knickers!'

'Honestly!' I said, sighing. 'I thought you tried to be hip, Dad. Everyone wears their skirts this length.'

It's true. Magda's skirt is even shorter. But her legs are long and lightly tanned. She's always moaning about her legs, saying she hates the way the muscle sticks out at the back. She used to do ballet and tap, and she still does jazz dancing. She moans but she doesn't mean it. She shows her legs off every chance she gets.

Nadine's skirts are short too. Her legs are never brown. They're either black when she's wearing her opaque tights or white when she has to go to school. Nadine can't stand getting sun-tanned. She's a very gothic girl with a vampire complexion. She's very willowy as well as white. Short skirts look so much better with slender legs.

It's depressing when your two best friends in all the world are much thinner than you are. It's even more depressing when your stepmother is thinner too. With positively model girl looks. Anna is only twenty-seven and she looks younger. When we go out together people think we're sisters. Only we don't look a bit alike. She's so skinny and striking. I'm little and lumpy.

I'm not exactly *fat*. Not really. It doesn't help having such a round face. Well, I'm round all over.

My tummy's round and my bum is round. Even my stupid *knees* are round. Still, my chest is round too. Magda has to resort to a Wonderbra to get a proper cleavage and Nadine is utterly flat.

I don't mind my top. I just wish there was much less of my bottom. Oh, God, what must I look like from the back view? No wonder he's staring.

I scuttle round the corner, feeling such a fool. My legs have gone so wobbly it's hard to walk. They look as if they're blushing too. Look at them, pink as hams. Who am I kidding? Of course I'm fat. The waistband on my indecently short skirt is uncomfortably tight. I've got fatter this summer, I just know I have. Especially these last three terrible weeks at the cottage.

It's so unfair. Everyone else goes off on these really glamorous jaunts abroad. Magda went to Spain. Nadine went to America. *I* went to our damp dreary cottage in Wales. And it rained and it rained and it rained. I got so bored sitting around playing infantile games of Snap and Old Maid with Eggs and watching fuzzy telly on the black-and-white portable and tramping through a sea of mud in my wellies that I just ate all the time.

Three meals a day, and at least thirty-three snacks. Mars bars and jelly beans and popcorn and tortilla chips and salt and vinegar crisps and Magnum ice-creams. Gobble gobble gobble, it's no wonder that I wobble. Yuck, my knees are actually wobbling as I walk.

I hate walking. I don't see the point of going for a walk, lumbering along in this great big loop just to get back to where you've come from. We always do so much walking in Wales.

Dad and Anna always stride ahead. Little Eggs leaps about like a loony. I slouch behind them, mud sucking at my wellies, and I think to myself: This is *fun*??? Why have a holiday cottage in Wales, of all places? Why can't we have a holiday villa in Spain or a holiday apartment in New York? Magda and Nadine are so *lucky*. OK, Magda was on a package tour and they stayed in a high-rise hotel and Nadine was only in Orlando doing a Disney, but I bet they both had brilliant sunshine every day.

In our little bit of Wales it's always the rainy season. Black clouds are a permanent fixture, like the mountains. It even rains *inside* the cottage because Dad thinks he can fix the roof slates himself and he always makes a total botch of it. We have buckets and bowls and saucepans scattered all over upstairs, and day and night there's this drip-tinkle-splosh symphony.

I got so utterly fed up and depressed that when we paid the usual visit to this boring old ruined castle I felt like casting myself off the battlements. I leaned against the stone wall at the top, my heart still banging away like crazy from the awful climb, and wondered what it would be like to leap over into thin air. Would anyone seriously care if I ended up going splat on the cobblestones below? Dad and Anna had a firm grip on Eggs but they didn't make a grab at me, even when I leaned right over, my head dangling.

They actually wandered off hand-in-hand with

him, mumbling about Bailies and Boiling Oil. They are overdoing the involved-parent act. I doubt if Eggs can spell castle yet so he's certainly not at the serious project stage. Dad never did all this stuff with me when I was little. He always seemed to be working or busy. When we went on holiday he went off sketching. But I didn't care. I had Mum. Then.

Thinking about Mum made me feel worse. People don't expect me to remember her still. They're mad. I can remember so much about her – heaps and heaps of stuff. The games we used to play with my Barbie dolls and the songs we'd sing and how she let me put on her make-up and try on all her jewellery and her pink silk petticoat and her high heels.

I want to talk about her so much but whenever I try with Dad he goes all tense and quiet. He frowns as if he has a headache. He doesn't want to remember Mum. Well, he's got Anna now. And they've both got Eggs.

I haven't got anyone. I started to feel so miserable I mooched off by myself. I walked to the other side of the battlements and found a crumbling turret. The entrance was roped off, with a warning. I ducked under the rope and climbed up all these dank steps in the dark. Then I put my foot on a step that wasn't there and tripped, banging my shin. It wasn't really that painful but I found I was crying. You can't really climb when you're crying, so I sat down and sobbed.

After a while I realized I didn't have a tissue. My glasses were all wet and my nose was running. I wiped and sniffed as best I could. The stone steps were very cold and the damp spread through my jeans but I still sat there. I suppose I was waiting for Dad to come looking for me. I waited and I waited and I waited. And then I heard footsteps. I sat still, listening. Quick, light footsteps. Too light for Dad. Too quick for me to get out of the way in time. Someone tripped right over me and we both screamed.

'Ouch!'

'Oooh!'

'I'm sorry, I didn't have a clue anyone was sitting there!'

'You're kneeling on me!'

'Sorry, sorry. Here, let me help you up.'

'Careful!' He was hauling so vigorously we both nearly toppled downwards.

'Whoops!'

'Watch out!'

I struggled free and stood with my back against the damp wall. He stood up too. It was too dark to make out more than a vague shape.

'What were you doing, sitting in the dark? You haven't hurt yourself, have you?'

'I wasn't hurt. I might be now. I still feel very squashed.'

'Sorry. I keep saying that, don't I? Though it *is* a bit crackers to crouch like that in the dark. Next time you might get a whole troop of boy scouts hiking over you. Or a coachload of American tourists trampling you with their trainers. Or . . . Or . . . I'm burbling. It's difficult making

18

conversation when you can't see. Let's go on up to see if it gets any lighter.'

'I don't think you can. The steps seem to give out.'

'Oh, well. That figures. Let's go back down then.'

I hesitated, having a quick wipe of my face with the back of my hand. There wasn't much point sitting there any longer. Dad and Anna and Eggs had probably forgotten all about me. Gone right back to the cottage. They'd suddenly snap their fingers three days later. 'What's happened to Ellie?' they'd say. And shrug. And forget about me again.

The boy seemed to think I was timid. 'I'll hold your hand if you like. To help you down.'

'I can manage perfectly, thanks,' I said.

Though it was a bit hairy feeling our way down. The steps seemed more slippery, and there wasn't any handrail. I stumbled once, and he grabbed me. 'Careful!'

'I'm *being* careful,' I said.

'I bet you there's an attendant waiting for us at the bottom to nag us rotten about the danger,' he said. 'That's the trouble, though. The minute I see something roped off I have this desperate urge to explore inside. So consequently I'm forever in a fix. Dopey Dan, that's what my family and friends call me when they're narked. I'm Daniel. But I'm only called that when they're really really really going ballistic. It's plain Dan most of the time.'

He went on like this until we emerged blinking into the daylight. Plain Dan was perfect. He had wild exploding hair and a silly little snub nose

19

that he twitched to hitch his glasses into place.

I blinked through my own smeary specs and focused properly.

'It's you!' we said simultaneously.

His family had another equally damp and dilapidated holiday cottage about half a mile down the valley from ours. We saw them in the village Spar buying their groceries and they were often in the pub in the evenings too. My dad and his dad sometimes played darts together. Anna and Dan's mum sat and made strained conversation. They looked like they came from different planets, even though they were both in jeans and jerseys and boots. Anna's jeans show off her tiny tight bum and her jersey is an Artwork designer sweater and her boots have got buckles and pointy toes. Dan's mum has a bum much bigger than mine. Her jumpers were all too tight, too, and one of them was actually unravelling. Her boots were serious walking boots caked with mud.

The whole family were serious walkers whatever the weather. We'd see them setting out in a downpour in their orange cagoules, and hours later we'd spot these mobile marigolds at the top of a dim distant mountain. There were five children, all earnest and old-fashioned. Dan was the eldest, about my age, a good inch shorter than me even though I'm little. He had a fat guidebook about castles sticking out of his cagoule. Typical.

'We made it!' he said, as if we'd just returned from outer space. He tried to jump the rope in triumph but tripped.

'No wonder they call you Dopey Dan,' I mumbled, as I skirted the rope.

There was still no sign of Dad and Anna and Eggs. Maybe they really *had* gone off without me.

'What's your name?' Dan asked, brushing himself down. 'Rapunzel?'

'*What?*'

'Well, I found you languishing in a tower, didn't I?'

I had sudden memories of a little Ladybird fairy-tale book. 'Are you into fairytales?' I said.

I intended it as an insult, but he took me seriously. 'I don't mind them actually. Some. My dad gave me a copy of *The Mabinogion*, seeing as we're in Wales.'

He could well have been speaking Welsh for all the sense he was making.

'It's old Welsh fairy stuff. Dead romantic in parts. I'll lend you the book if you like.'

'I don't think it sounds my sort of thing.'

'So what is your sort of thing, eh? What do you like reading? What's that little black book you've always got with you?'

I was surprised. He must have been watching me carefully. I usually kept my book hidden in my jacket pocket. 'That's just my little sketchbook.'

'Let's have a look then,' he said, patting my pocket.

'No!'

'Go on, don't be shy.'

'I'm not the slightest bit shy. It's *private*.'

'What sort of thing do you sketch? Castles?'

'*Not* castles.'

21

'Mountains?'

'Not mountains either.'

'Then what?'

'God, you aren't half nosy.'

He wrinkled his snub nose at me cheerfully.

I gave in. 'I don't sketch. I draw. Stylized pictures. Cartoons.'

'Oh, great. I love that sort of stuff. Do you ever do comic strips? I love Calvin and Hobbes. And Asterix, I've got all those books. Look, I've even got Snowy on my socks.' He hitched up his jeans and straightened his socks, which were all bunched up in his Woollies trainers.

'Very cute,' I said.

He grinned. 'OK, OK. I know my clothes aren't exactly hip.'

He was dead right there. If I was home I'd be terrified of being seen talking to him. But he was kind of fun in a silly lollopy way, as persistent as a puppy. He didn't even seem to mind my being so snappy with him. I wouldn't normally have been anywhere near as sharp. It was just I was getting seriously bothered about my stupid family.

His family were all down in the grounds, peering knowledgeably at little heaps of stones. One of his sisters looked up and spotted us. 'Hey, Dan! Come on down, we need your castle book!'

All the other little marigolds waved and shouted.

'I'd better get cracking. They won't stop now they've started,' said Dan. 'You coming?'

I followed him down. Dad and Anna and Eggs weren't anywhere. Maybe I'd have to join up with the marigolds. I was getting so desperate that it began to seem an attractive idea.

But guess who I came across strolling round outside the castle walls. Dad and Anna and Eggs. They didn't look the slightest bit concerned.

'Hi, Ellie,' said Dad. 'Hey, have you made a friend? Great.'

Dan grinned. I glared.

'Where have you been?' I demanded.

'Well, we were showing Eggs the way medieval people went to the loo in the castle – and then he needed to go himself so we had to trail right over to the toilets. Oh, poor Ellie, were you getting worried?'

'No, of course not,' I said sulkily.

'See you around . . . Ellie,' said Dan.

I did see him around a few times after that. Mostly with the marigolds. And Eggs. One day we joined up for a picnic. It even drizzled that day so we ate damp sandwiches and soggy sausages and mushy crisps. No-one else seemed to find this depressing. Dan was especially good at keeping all the little ones amused. Eggs *adored* him. I got sick of all this clowning around and went and sat on a wet rock and drew.

I was doodling away when a shadow fell across my page. I snapped my book shut.

'Let me see,' said Dan.

'No.'

'Meanie. Go on, special favour. Seeing as it's the last day of the hols.'

'Thank God.'

23

'What?'

'I can't stick this dump.'

'You're mad. It's fantastic. And anyway, who wants to go back home? School on Monday. Yuck yuck yuck. I wonder what it'll be like – in Year Nine.'

'You're not going to be in Year Nine,' I said. I'd found out that Dan was only *twelve*. Not even a teenager yet.

'Yes, I am.'

'Rubbish. You'll be in Year Eight. With the other little boys.'

'I *am* going to be in Year Nine. Honest.' Dan looked unusually embarrassed. 'I've been put up a year, right?'

'Oh, God. Because you're so brainy?'

'You've got it.'

'Trust you! I should have sussed you out for a right swot.'

'You ought to be pleased you're going out with a boy of mega-brainpower,' said Dan.

'We're not going *out*, idiot.'

'I wish we could.'

'What?'

'I like you, Ellie,' he said seriously. 'Will you be my girlfriend?'

'No! Of course not. You're just a baby.'

'Don't you fancy having a toy-boy?'

'Definitely not!'

'Can't I see you sometimes?'

'You're nuts, Dan. You live in Manchester, I live in London, right?'

'Can we write to each other then?'

He nagged on until I gave in and scribbled my address on a page torn from my sketchbook. He's probably lost it already, knowing Dan. Not that I *want* to know him. He won't bother writing even if he's still got the address. And even if he does I don't think I'll reply. There's no point. I mean, he's just this irritating little kid. I suppose he's OK in small doses. But he's not exactly boyfriend material.

Oh dear. If only he were five years older! And not all nerdy and nutty. Why can't he be really cool, with fantastic fair hair and dark brown eyes???

I wonder if I'll see that blond boy again tomorrow. I slow down, going all dreamy just thinking about him. Then I catch sight of my face in a shop window. I look like I'm brain-dead, eyes glazed, mouth open. And then I see the clock at the back of the shop and it's gone nine. Gone nine! It can't be. It *is*!

Gone nine, number nine, my first day in Year Nine – and I'm going to be in trouble before I've even started.

Nine Heroes and Heroines

1 JOHN LENNON - because he was the best Beatle, a funny artist, and he wanted to give peace a chance.

2 FRIDA KAHLO - because she produced amazing paintings lying flat on her back in terrible pain.

3 ANNE FRANK - because she wrote a wonderful diary hiding in that annexe in Amsterdam during the war.

4 VAN GOGH - because he was such a great artist and went on painting even though he never sold a single canvas.

5 ANNE RICE - because she writes about vampires and has a huge house full of life-size china dolls.

6 MAURICE SENDAK - because his drawings are incredible, especially 'Where the Wild Things Are.'

7 JULIAN CLARY - because he's so outrageous and I think he's ever so good looking.

8 ZOE BALL - because she's so bubbly and I used to like watching her art programme.

ART ATTACK

9 NICK PARK - because Wallace and Gromit are fantastic!

Two Best Friends

It's weird walking along the corridor to Mrs Henderson's room. We *would* have to have Mrs Hockeysticks Henderson as our class tutor in Year Nine. What *is* it about Games teachers? She's always picked on me right from Year Seven.

'Come *along*, Eleanor!'

'Missed *again*, Eleanor.'

'You're not even running, girl, get a *move on!*'

I developed strategic tactics, suddenly stricken with appalling migraines or agonizing periods at the start of every Games lesson, but she soon got wise to me. She made me run six times round the hockey pitch for malingering and blew her poxy whistle at me whenever I tried to slow down.

I can't stick Mrs Henderson. I've always hated PE. Magda sometimes hangs about with me and acts like she's useless too. She doesn't like games either. She hates to get her hair blown about and she won't try to catch a ball in case she breaks a nail. Yet if she's forced to participate she can run like the wind, shoot six goals in a row at netball and whack a hockey ball clear across the pitch.

At least Nadine is even more hopeless than me. She looks graceful but when she's forced to run her arms and legs jerk out at odd angles and she totters along like a broken puppet, her head hanging.

I can't *wait* to see Magda and Nadine. I haven't seen them for weeks. We only got back from that stupid crumbling cottage yesterday. But somehow my feet are going more and more s-l-o-w-l-y as they squeak along the newly polished corridor. They look so hideous too, regulation brown school shoes, you've never seen such rubbish, your actual Clarks clodhoppers, when at any other school girls can wear whatever they want – heels, trainers, Doc Martens . . . Oh, there are these seriously wonderful sexy shoes in Shelleys! OK, they've got heels, *high* heels, but they're this amazing shiny bronze colour. Now bronze is brown. Well, brownish. I begged Anna to let me have them for school but she wouldn't give in. It's so unfair. Just because she wears those boring Sloaney little pumps all the time. She's one inch taller than Dad and ever so self-conscious about it.

'Eleanor Allard?'

Oh, God. It's Miss Trumper, the deputy head. She's even worse than Mrs Henderson. School's only started five minutes and she's already on the warpath. It's pathetic. Why can't these old bags get a *life*?

'What are you doing lurking in the corridor, Eleanor?'

'Nothing, Miss Trumper.'

'I can see that for myself. Whose class are you in this year?'

'Mrs Henderson's,' I say, nodding at the door right in front of me.

'Well, why are you just standing there? You don't mean to tell me you've been sent out the classroom in disgrace *already*?'

'No! I haven't even gone in there yet.'

'Well, do so, Eleanor. At once!'

I seize the door handle. I can hear Mrs Henderson in full flow inside, giving the class an introduction to the 1001 rules that must never be broken in Class Nine Neptune. Oh, yeah — all the years are divided into these pathetic planets: Venus, Mars, Mercury and Neptune. Funny how they never pick Uranus. We're Neptune and we have this little trident thing on our badges. It's all so boring. None of us want to be in Neptune anyway. Magda fancies Venus and Nadine wants to be in Mars because she likes the chocolate bars and I want to be in Mercury because I've got a soft spot for the late lamented Freddie . . .

'Eleanor!' Miss Trumper has paused halfway along the corridor. 'Have you gone into a catatonic trance?'

Dear goodness, they think they're so *witty*.

'No, Miss Trumper.'

'Then go into your classroom!'

I take a deep breath and turn the handle. In I go. And there's Mrs Henderson, sitting on her table swinging her legs. She's wearing a yucky pleated skirt to show she's being class tutor, but she's got bare legs and ankle socks and tennis shoes so she's all set to bounce off down to the gym when she's finished giving everyone an earful first lesson.

I get two earfuls. In fact she gets so aerated that my poor ears expand to Dumbo proportions. Stuff like *First Day*. And *Idleness* and *Attitude*. And *Just Not Good Enough*.

I bow my head and act like I'm in the depths of despair just to disconcert her. Under my hair I peer round for Magda and Nadine. Great, they're right at the back! Magda's grinning at me. Nadine gives me a little wave. They've saved me the seat in between them. And *eventually* Mrs Henderson draws breath and lets me slide off to the back. Magda whispers 'Hi, babe,' and Nadine gives me some chewing gum and I settle down and school is started. At least old Henderson didn't give me a detention for being late the first day!

First days are always so bitty. There's all the new timetables and notebooks and each and every teacher starts in on their own little lecture about Now You're in Year Nine. Then at morning break Chrissie shows us all these photos she took in Barbados during the holidays and then Jess has us all in fits telling us about this action holiday she went on where she did this bungee-jumping and she keeps trying to demonstrate – so we don't have a

31

moment's peace to be just *us*, Magda-Nadine-and-Ellie, until after lunch.

We saunter off to our special place on the steps that lead down to the Portakabins. It's where the three of us have always sat for the last two years. But there's a whole bunch of drippy little new kids hanging around doing handstands up against the wall, skirts tucked into their brand-new regulation ghastly grey school knickers.

'Per-lease,' says Magda. 'Can't you kiddiwinks go and wave your legs somewhere else? It's just too distracting, dearies.'

They straighten up, giggling foolishly, and then scatter when Magda flaps her hands at them.

'Right,' she says, seating herself carefully. Her skirt is a good six centimetres shorter than mine. She has to position it with extreme accuracy or else *she'll* be the one showing off her knickers. Which are definitely *not* regulation.

Nadine sits beside her, kicking off her battered school shoes. I can see her black pearl toenail varnish through her tights.

I nudge up beside them, feeling a sudden warm rush of love for both of them.

Nadine's been my friend ever since nursery school, when we stirred bright green dough in the Wendy House and played we were poisoning all the dollies. We stayed staunch friends all through primary school, playing Witches in the playground and Mermaids when we went swimming and Ghosts when we spent the night at each other's houses. We vowed we would stay best friends for ever and ever, just the two of us. But the first year of secondary school we weren't allowed to sit where we wanted. We had to be in alphabetical order. I found myself sitting next to Magda.

I was a bit scared of Magda at first. Even when she was only eleven she had a proper figure and she arranged her hair in a very sophisticated style and wore a thick coat of mascara so that her eyes looked knowing. She had finely plucked eyebrows that she raised when she took a second look at you.

She hardly spoke to me that first week. Then one time in class I was doodling on the back of my new school roughbook, drawing an ultra-hip cool-cat Magda. I made her a real pussycat with sharp whiskers and a fluffy tail. I drew me as a little fat mouse, frightened of Magda, all twitchy nose and scrabbly paws. Magda suddenly leant over me to see what I was doing. She worked it out at once. 'Hey, Ellie! That's *great*,' she said.

So I drew some more stuff and she liked that too. We were friends after that. She wanted me to be her *best* friend.

Only of course I had Nadine. And Nadine didn't like Magda at all at first. But when Magda invited me over to her place one day after school I forced Nadine to come too. I wanted moral support more than anything else. I imagined Magda living this amazing cool independent existence. I couldn't have been more wrong. She's got this lovely noisy interfering funny family. Magda's the baby. Everyone's pet. She acts like a cute little kid at home. Anyway, she invited Nadine and me up to her bedroom and she gave us both a full make-up job. I loved it. She actually made me look like I had big dark eyes behind my specs and she did this subtle line each side of my face so it looked like I had cheekbones. It was the first time I'd ever worn make-up and I thought it was wonderful. Nadine was a bit sniffy. Magda said it was her turn. She gave Nadine a real gothic look, chalk-white face and truly black lipstick and astonishing outlined eyes. When Nadine saw herself in the mirror she smiled all over her amazing new face and wanted Magda to be her friend too.

So we've been this best-friend threesome ever since, right through Years Seven and Eight. Now we're Year Nine, thirteen — well, Magda's nearly fourteen, and Nadine is fourteen in December, but I've got to wait all the way round till next June.

It's irritating. I really look the youngest now, because I'm still so small and roly-poly with these revoltingly chubby cheeks. I have *dimples*, for goodness' sake. I'm used to Magda looking older, especially now she's highlighted her hair. But Nadine used to look really young for her age with her heart-shaped face and her long black hair tumbling round her shoulders like an Alice in negative. Now she looks . . . different.

'Come on, then, I haven't seen you both for ages! What have you been up to?' says Magda, but she doesn't pause for breath. She tells Nadine and me all about her Spanish holiday, and how all these waiters kept waylaying her and this guy at the pool kept picking her up and throwing her in the water and this other much older guy kept trying to buy her drinks at the poolside . . . This is the standard Magda stuff and I don't always concentrate because I'm watching Nadine. She doesn't look as if she's listening either, bending forward so that her hair hides her face like a black velvet curtain. She's inking a tattoo on her wrist with a black felt-tip pen, a careful heart with an elaborate inked frill. This is a change for Nadine. Her tattoos are usually skulls or spiders.

'What about you, Nadine?' I say the second Magda shuts up.

'*What* about me?' says Nadine. 'You mean my hols? I saw you after. Before you went to your cottage. It was hell. Relentlessly cheery. And you had to queue for hours and all the kids had Mickey Mouse ears and there were all these giant cartoon characters *waving* at everyone. It was all so bright. It made my eyes ache.'

'Crawl back to your coffin, Ms Vampire,' says Magda, laughing. 'I bet Natasha loved it.'

Natasha is Nadine's little sister. Nadine and I have never been able to stand her, but Magda is extraordinary, she actually likes little kids. She's even fond of Eggs. She's always going on about how she'd like to have little brothers and sisters herself.

'Natasha ate four ice-creams and then was very sick all down her brand-new pink Minnie Mouse T-shirt,' says Nadine. She painstakingly inks a name across her heart.

I lean forward to read it. 'Liam?' I say.

Nadine blushes. Nadine *never* blushes — she doesn't look as if she's got enough blood — but now

I can see bright pink beneath the fronds of black hair.

'Liam?' says Magda. 'I didn't know you were an Oasis fan.'

'Not *that* Liam,' says Nadine.

Magda looks at me for enlightenment. I shake my head. We both turn back to Nadine.

'So who's *this* Liam then?' Magda asks.

'Oh,' says Nadine. A tiny pause. 'He's my boyfriend.'

We stare at her. 'Your *boyfriend*?'

I nearly tip over backwards down the steps. Nadine has a boyfriend. I can't believe it! How come Nadine's got a boyfriend before me? Before *Magda*? Magda has loads of guys fawning all over her – well, so she says – but she doesn't actually go *out* with anyone yet.

'A *real* boyfriend?' says Magda, and she sounds just as shocked as me.

'But you don't even *like* boys, Nadine,' I say.

'I like Liam,' says Nadine. 'And he isn't a boy anyway. Not really. He's seventeen. At college.'

'So where did you meet him?' says Magda, sounding suspicious. 'How come you've never even mentioned him before?'

'Yes, you didn't say a thing about this Liam in your letters, Nad,' I say.

I wrote lots of letters to Nadine and Magda when I was cooped up in the cottage. Magda never bothers to write back properly. She just sends postcards with 'Love and Kisses, Magda' on the back – which is sweet, but not exactly informative.

Nadine is a much more satisfactory correspondent

– several pages in her carefully printed italic script, with little showers of star and moon sequins scattered inside the envelope. But all she wrote about was this weird new band she's keen on and how she's trying to teach herself to read the Tarot and a whole long moan about her family. Her dad's forever on at her to work harder even though she's always in the top three at school. He can't see why she can't come top in everything, which is crazy because Amna is always way in front of everyone and she's got this mega IQ, like she's a total genius and no-one could ever beat her no matter how hard they tried. Then her mum hates Nadine's clothes and make-up and hairstyle and wants her to smarten up and wear these chichi clothes and smile like an American cheerleader. And Natasha is just Awfulness in Ankle Socks, acting the Angel Child whenever Mummy and Daddy are around but being the Brat from Hell whenever Nadine is forced to look after her.

So, there was all the usual stuff but not a single line about a Liam. I can't help feeling outraged. Nadine and I always tell each other *everything*. 'Why didn't you *tell* me?' I say. My voice cracks, almost as if I'm going to start crying.

'I've only just met him,' says Nadine, stretching her arm out to admire her completed love-token tattoo.

'Ah!' says Magda, her eyebrows arching. 'So he's just this guy you've seen around, right? Not an *actual* boyfriend?'

'An "I wish" boyfriend,' I say, cheering up

considerably, getting all set to tell them about the blond guy I saw coming to school this morning.

'No, no. Liam and I went out together Saturday night,' says Nadine. 'We met in Tower Records that morning. I was sorting through the indie section and he was too, and we were both looking for the same band and there was just the one CD so he said I could have it.'

'And then he asked you out, just like that?' I say incredulously.

'Well . . . we chatted a bit. *He* did. I couldn't think of a thing to say, actually. I was just standing there dying, wishing I could come out with something, *anything*. Then he started asking me about this other group who had a gig at the Wily Fox that night and he said did I want to go. So I said yes. Though I've never been to the Wily Fox. Well, *any* pub. You know my mum and dad, they'd go crazy if they ever found out, so when I got back I said you'd got back from the cottage early, Ellie, and we were both going round to Magda's for this little party, and then your dad was going to take me home. I had to say that, because I guessed I'd be back really late from the Wily Fox. I hope you don't mind.'

'So you went there on your own?' I say, astonished. I still can't believe it. Nadine's always so quiet. She generally stays shut up in her bedroom playing her loopy music night after night. She never goes anywhere.

'And he turned up OK, this Liam?' says Magda.

'I didn't think he would. I was so scared of going

in there by myself. I was sure they'd chuck me out for being under age,' says Nadine.

'Why didn't you phone me? I'd have come with you,' says Magda.

'Yes, but it might have put him off. Or he might have liked you better than me,' says Nadine.

Magda nods.

'No, I thought I'd just put my head round the door and have a look and then I could always run home if I wanted. But he was there before me and he paid for us to go into the back room where the band were playing and then he took me home after. Well, to the end of the road. I didn't dare let him come further in case my mum and dad saw. And then I'm seeing him again *next* Saturday so can I say I'm spending it with you, Ellie?'

'Yeah. Sure,' I say, still stunned.

'So what's he *like*?' says Magda.

'Oh, he's really cool. Dark hair, moody dark eyes, hip clothes.'

'Did you tell him how old you are?' I ask.

'Not at first. I made out I was fifteen. And he said "Nearly old enough",' says Nadine, giggling.

'Oh, God,' says Magda.

'Yeah, OK, but later I was talking about you two, and I said I'd been friends with Ellie for ever and friends with Magda the two years we'd been in secondary school, and then I realized what I'd said. And Liam twigged – but he just teased me a bit. He doesn't mind that I'm only thirteen. Well, nearly fourteen. He says I act old for my age, actually.'

'I see,' says Magda. 'So. Did you snog?'

39

'Yes. Lots.'

'Did he open his mouth?'

'Of course,' says Nadine. 'He's a truly great kisser.'

My own mouth is open. Nadine and I have frequently discussed French kissing and we both thought it a squirmily revolting idea, someone else's sluggy tongue slithering around your fillings.

'You said—' I start.

Nadine giggles. 'Yes, but it's different with Liam.'

'It's great, isn't it?' says Magda, who has given us frequent accounts of her own amorous encounters.

Nadine is looking at me almost pityingly. 'You'll see, Ellie,' she says. 'When you get a proper boyfriend of your own.'

That's it.

My mouth stays open and starts talking. 'Oh, don't worry, I've *got* a boyfriend,' I say, before I can stop myself.

Nadine stares at me.

Magda stares at me.

It's like I've nipped out around my glasses and *I'm* staring at me too.

What have I just said???

What am I doing?

How come I started this?

But I can't stop now . . .

Nine Wishes

1. I wish I really had a boyfriend.

2. I wish I was a stone lighter. No - two stone.

3. I wish I was six inches taller.

4. I wish I had long blond silky hair.

5. I wish I had a leather jacket.

6. I wish I had new shoes from Shelleys.

7. I wish I was eighteen.

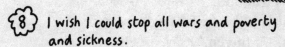

lighter

taller

older

8. I wish I could stop all wars and poverty and sickness.

9. I wish I still had my mum.

Three Boyfriends

I hear this voice going on about a boy on holiday in Wales. A boy I kept seeing – but I didn't get a chance to talk to him until we met up in a romantic ruined castle one wild and windy day. 'We literally fell into each other's arms!' I say.

Well, it's sort of true.

I tell them he's called Dan. They immediately ask how old he is.

'He's not as old as your Liam, Nad,' I say.

That's true too.

'So how old *is* he?' Magda insists.

'He's . . . fifteen,' I say.

He *will* be, in three years' time.

'What does he look like? Is he dishy? What sort of clothes does he wear?' Magda persists.

I abandon all attempt at truth. 'He's very good

42

looking. Blond. His hair's lovely, it sort of comes forward in a wavy fringe, just a little bit tousled. He's got dark eyes, a really intense brown. He's got this way of looking at you . . . He's just a real dream. His clothes are very casual, nothing too posey. Jeans, sweatshirt – still, that's just what he was wearing on holiday. It's so unfair, we didn't meet up properly until right at the end, and yet somehow when we started talking it was like we'd known each other for ever, you know?'

'Did he kiss you?' Nadine asks.

'We didn't get a chance to kiss, worst luck. We were with my stupid family nearly all the time. We *did* manage to steal off together at a picnic, but just as Dan was getting really romantic, Eggs came chasing over to us and started pestering us and that was it! *Honestly!*'

'What are you getting all passionate about, Eleanor?'

Oh, God, it's Mrs Henderson in her tracksuit, jogging off to the gym.

I look down at my lap, going all pink, trying desperately hard not to giggle.

'Her boyfriend!' says Magda.

'Surprise, surprise!' says Mrs Henderson. She sighs. 'You girls seem to discuss little else. You've all got one-track minds. Many thousands of determined intelligent women fought battles throughout this century to broaden your horizons, and yet you'd sooner sit there babbling about boys than concentrate on your all-round education.'

'You said it, Mrs Henderson,' says Magda. Unwisely.

'Well, you three are going to have to curtail your cosy little chat and do a detention tomorrow, because you've been so carried away by your enthralling conversation that you've failed to notice the bell for afternoon school went five minutes ago. Now get to your lessons at *once*!'

We jump to it. We get told off all over again when we get to English. It isn't fair. I quite like English. It's about the only thing I'm any good at, apart from Art, but now Mrs Madley glares at us and goes on and on and we get divided up and I have to sit right at the front.

We're doing *Romeo and Juliet* this year. Everyone thinks it's dead boring. Privately I quite like Shakespeare. I like the way the words go, though I don't understand half of it. Certainly the beginning bit's dull – but when I flip through the book and find the first Juliet part it gets much more interesting. Juliet is only thirteen, nearly fourteen, so *she'd* be in Year Nine too. As far as I can work out her mother and her nurse are keen for her to get *married*.

I sit wondering what it would be like to be married at thirteen in Juliet's day. It would be fun as long as you were rich enough to have someone pay the mortgage on your Italian mansion and loads of servants to spruce up your medieval Versace frocks and deliver your pizzas to your marital fourposter . . .

Mrs Madley suddenly shouts my name, making me jump. 'You not only come to my lesson ten minutes late, Eleanor Allard, but you obviously aren't paying the slightest attention now you're here! What on earth is the matter with you?'

'She's in love, Mrs Madley,' says Magda. She can't *ever* keep her mouth shut.

Mrs Madley groans in exasperation while the whole class collapses.

It looks like I'm in serious trouble *again*. I stare wildly at the page in front of me. I spot a line at the top that looks dead appropriate ' "Under love's heavy burden do I sink",' I quote, sending myself up.

Mrs Madley is wrong-footed. She even looks mildly amused. 'Well, take care you don't sink too far, Eleanor. Look what happens to these star-crossed lovers at the end of the play. Now, girls, settle down, and let us *all* concentrate on Shakespeare.'

I decide I'd better concentrate too – so I don't really have time to plan what on earth I'm going to say going home from school with Magda and Nadine.

In Maths last lesson there's no point my trying to concentrate because I can't figure any of it out, so I sit nibbling my thumbnail, worrying about this boyfriend situation. When I was little I used to suck my thumb a lot. Now when I'm ultra-anxious I find I have to have a little weeny suck and chew just to calm myself. I wondered if smoking might have the same effect – not in a classroom situation obviously – but when Magda shared a packet of Benson's with me I felt so sick and dizzy by the time I lit up my second it's put me off for life.

I have to sort out what I'm going to say about Dan. I think of his blond hair and dark brown eyes . . . Only that's the boy I saw this morning on the way to school. I don't even have a clue who he is. I just started describing him when Magda and Nadine asked all those questions. I couldn't tell them what the real Dan looks like or they'd crease up laughing.

Oh, God, *why* did I open my big mouth? I was like some demented Fairy Godmother waving a wand over nerdy little boy Dopey Dan in Wales and turning him into the Golden Dream I saw this morning.

Magda and Nadine believe it all too. *I* practically believe it. I've always had this crazy habit of making things up. It was mostly when I was little. Like after my mum died . . .

It was so horrible and lonely that I kept trying to pretend she wasn't *really* dead, that if I could only perform all these really loopy tasks like go all day without going to the toilet or stay awake an entire night then suddenly she'd come walking into my bedroom and it would all be a mistake, someone else's mother had died, not *mine*. Sometimes when I was lying awake holding my eyelids open I'd almost believe she was really there, standing by my bed, leaning over ready to give me a cuddle, so close I could actually smell her lovely soft powdery scent.

Even after I gave up on those daft tricks I didn't give up on my mother. I felt she still had to be around for me. I talked to her inside my head and she talked back, saying all the ordinary Mum things, telling me to be careful crossing the road, and to eat up like a good girl, and when I went to bed she'd chat to me about my day and she'd always say 'Nightie Nightie' and I'd whisper 'Pyjama Pyjama'. I did that long after Dad married Anna. She said some of that stuff too, but it wasn't the same at all. I used to hate Anna simply because she wasn't Mum. I'm older now. I can see it's not really Anna's fault. She's OK, sometimes. But she's still *not* my mum.

So what would Mum say? This is the awful bit. I can still make Mum say all this stuff to me, but it's the *old* stuff that I needed to hear when I was little. My made-up mum can't seem to get her head round the idea that I'm big now. Big enough to want a boyfriend. Only I haven't *got* one and yet I've told my two best friends I have.

'Tell them the truth, Ellie,' Mum says firmly, her voice suddenly loud and clear.

She sounds so real I actually look round the class-room to see if anyone else can hear her.

I know Mum is right. In fact I even work out how to do it. I shall say I was just teasing them, playing a silly joke to see how much they'd swallow. I'll say I did meet a boy called Dan on holiday but I'll say what he's *really* like. I'll even tell them about the gorgeous blond bloke on the way to school. I'll draw a cartoon for them, the real Dan and me with my wand turning him into the Dreamboat. They'll think it's funny. Well – maybe more funny peculiar than funny ha-ha. But they're used to me being a bit weird. They'll still *like* me, even though they'll think I'm nuttier than ever.

I'll tell them on the way to the bus stop. Then it'll be over and everything will go back to normal. Except Nadine really *has* got a boyfriend. This Liam. Unless . . . could *she* have made him up too? Nadine and I used to play all these pretend games together. She was always great at making things up, that's why I always wanted her for my friend. Oh, what a hoot if Nadine's been fibbing too! I really wouldn't put it past her!

But when we come out of school at the end of lessons and Magda is asking me more about Dan and I'm all set to say my piece, though my throat's dry with nerves and I feel incredibly silly, Nadine suddenly stops dead and gasps.

'Nadine?'

We stare at her. She's blushing. I can't get used to seeing Nadine's snowy skin shine salmon-pink.

'Nadine, what's up?' I say.

Magda is quicker than me. She's seen what Nadine is staring at. Not what. *Who.* 'Wow!' says Magda. 'Is he Liam?'

Nadine swallows. 'Yes! Oh, God, what am I going to do? I'm in my school *uniform.*'

'Well, he knows you go to school.'

'But I look such a berk in uniform. I can't let him see me like this!' Nadine dodges behind me, ducking right down. 'Walk backwards into school, Ellie!' she hisses.

'Don't be so nuts, Nadine,' says Magda. 'Look, he's seen you anyway.'

'How do you know?' Nadine mutters, still hiding behind me.

'Because he's waving like crazy over in our direction. And he's not waving at me. Worse luck. He's really gorgeous,' says Magda.

He is. He's tall and he's got dark hair and very dark eyes and he looks hip in his skimpy black top and black jeans. He's the sort of guy who seems totally out of our class. Like my blond dreamboat. But Liam isn't pretend. He's real and he's still waving at Nadine.

She steps sideways round me, pink and pretty. It's as if she's a whole new person who I hardly know. She waves back, an odd little waggle of her fingers, her elbow tucked into her side. Then she runs over to the wall where he's waiting.

'I can't believe it,' Magda mutters. 'He's so yummy. What does he see in Nadine?'

'Magda! Don't be such a bitch,' I say primly – but she's only saying out loud what I'm thinking.

I feel as if I've been in a race with Nadine and I always thought I'd win, but now she's forged ahead and left me behind.

'Come on, Ellie, let's go and say hello,' says Magda.

'No! We can't butt in.'

'Of course we can,' says Magda, shoving me sharply in their direction. She runs one hand through her hair, fluffing it up, and undoes the top button of her school blouse. 'Hey, Nadine,' she calls, wiggling across the playground towards them.

I stand foolishly, not sure whether to follow. I edge towards them as if I'm playing Grandmother's Footsteps. Nadine is sitting on the wall beside Liam.

Magda is standing in front of them, one hand on her hip. She's chatting away like crazy but it doesn't look as if Liam is paying her much attention. Nadine isn't saying much. She's looking down, hiding behind her hair.

'Oh, and this is my other friend, Ellie,' she mumbles when I get near.

What's wrong with her voice? She sounds all wet and whispery.

'Hello,' I say awkwardly.

Liam gives me a curt nod and turns back to Nadine. 'You look cute in the uniform,' he says.

'I look *awful*,' Nadine protests. 'What are you doing here anyway?'

'I finished early at college so I thought I'd see if I could spot you amongst all your little schoolgirly chums. So come on. Let's go for a walk or something.'

'OK,' says Nadine, swinging her legs over the wall.

Liam raises his eyebrows and she giggles stupidly.

''Bye then, Nadine. 'Bye, Liam,' says Magda. She waves. He doesn't bother to respond.

'Well!' says Magda, staring after them. 'So we're the little schoolgirly chums, eh, Ellie?'

'She's so different with him,' I mutter.

'He doesn't exactly get ten out of ten in the charm stakes,' says Magda. 'I hope Nadine knows what she's doing. He's ever so old for her.'

'I don't like him,' I say.

'Neither do I. Though if he'd liked *me* more I might feel more positive,' says Magda, laughing.

That's one thing about Magda. She might be a real scheming bitch at times but she's always honest about it.

'Oh well, Ellie, I'll walk with you to the bus stop, eh?'

She links her arm in mine. There's a whole crowd of Anderson boys at the bus stop. Our school is Anderson High School too, but they're entirely separate, across the road from each other on different sites. One school for girls, one school for boys. Twin schools for separate sexes. Only most of the Anderson boys are so awful it's depressing. The little ones are just like animals, yelling and kicking and bashing each other with their schoolbags. Their idea of sophisticated humour is farting. Come to think of it, the Year Nines go in for that a lot too. They are all revolting, each and every one. The Year Tens and Elevens are almost as bad, though I suppose there are a few possibles.

One of these possibles is at the bus stop. He's Greg Someone. I suppose he's quite good looking but he's got red hair that he hates, so he puts heaps of gel on it to make it as dark as he can. If you were ever in a clinch with Greg and you ran your fingers through his hair it would be like dabbling in cold chip fat. *Not* a happy thought.

Magda's never given him a second glance before, but suddenly she bounces up to him. 'Hey, Greg. How's things? Did you have a good holiday? Pretty dire having to come back to this old dump, eh? And look at all this homework first day back, can you believe it! See how heavy my bag is.' She thrusts it

51

at Greg. He staggers, blinking rapidly. It's not the heaviness of Magda's bag. It's the heaviness of her approach. I don't think she's ever said one *word* to him before.

He turns almost as red as his hair and looks totally idiotic. Magda gazes at Belisha Beacon boy as if he's a Keanu or a Brad. She sighs and stretches her arms, making out they're aching. This action has an amazing effect on her school blouse. The buttons strain. Greg positively *glows*.

A foul little gang of Year Eights are ogling too, nudging each other and making disgusting comments. Magda shakes her head at them. She makes a pithy comment that indicates they have been exercising their own arms more than some-what. Then she looks back at Greg. Her blue eyes have a positively lighthouse beam. 'You're not any good at Maths, are you, Greg? I'm *useless*.'

She's not, actually. I'm the one who can't even add up correctly using a calculator. Nadine's not much better. Magda is always the girl who does *our* Maths homework, but now she's acting like she's got candy floss for a brain.

'I'm OK at Maths actually,' says Greg. 'What's the problem then?'

'Oh, it's ever so complicated,' says Magda. 'And look, isn't that the bus coming? I don't get on the bus, I'm just here with my friend. Look Greg, do you ever go to the McDonald's near the market?'

'Sure I do.'

'Well, how about if we meet up there? Half seven, something like that? And I'll bring my stupid Maths with me and see if you can make me understand it, OK?'

'Yes, sure,' said Greg. 'Half seven. Right.'

'It's a date,' says Magda, retrieving her schoolbag and giving Greg a dazzling smile. She turns to me – and winks.

So now Magda's got herself a boyfriend too. In less than five minutes.

Greg waves after her as he gets on the bus. I wonder if he might sit next to me as I'm Magda's friend, but he barges straight past and sits with some other Anderson boys who have already got on. He's talking rapidly, obviously showing off that he's scored with Magda.

I sit all by myself. I am starting to feel seriously depressed. So. I didn't tell Magda and Nadine I was making it all up. I didn't get a chance, did I? And Nadine has got a real boyfriend. And now Magda has got one too, just like that. Why can't *I* chat someone up the way she can?

I gaze round the bus in desperation. There are two nerdy Year Ten Anderson boys sitting across the way from me, earnestly discussing some stupid sci-fi stuff. They look like beings from another planet themselves but I'm so desperate I'll try anything.

I bare my teeth at them in a big cheesy grin. They reel back as if I'm a rabid dog about to bite. I cover my teeth and cower in my seat. It's no use. I'm not like Magda.

Oh, God, I feel so fed up. I'm never ever going to get a boyfriend. No boy in the entire world is ever going to fancy me.

No. I am wrong. When I get home there is a letter waiting for me.

Nine Things I **Hate** About School

1. It starts too early.

2. The teachers - ESPECIALLY Mrs Henderson and Miss Trumper.

3. Maths - yuck.
4. PE - even yuckier.
5. The sarcastic way the teachers tell you off.
6. The bitchy way girls whisper behind your back.

7. Having to rush everywhere and getting all sweaty.
8. The worry about the pale grey school skirt the first day of your period.

9. Homework - and we have such HEAPS now we're in Year Nine.

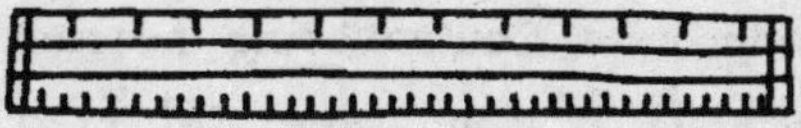

Four in the Family

Dear Ellie,

Hello! It's me, Dan. Sorry this is such jiggly writing. I'm scribbling this going home in the car and various sprogs keep jogging me and my mum is driving and she's a total maniac - she does a ninety-mile-an-hour dash down the motorway and then when one of the kids starts screaming for a wee she screeches to a halt on the hard shoulder in seconds so that we practically hurtle through the windscreen.

This is not romantic subject matter for a love letter. OK, shall I try to be romantic? I should make up a super romantic fable about a fair maiden languishing in a tower being rescued by a handsome knight. A Welsh fable, set in a Welsh castle. Like THE MABINOGION. That's those old Welsh tales I told you about. They're written down in a White book and a Red book. Well, this isn't a book, it's a scrappy letter, and you're not fair, you're dark, and I'm not handsome. You can say that again. I know you think I'm all nerdy and nutty. Well, I'm wordy as well as nerdy. And OK, who cares if I'm nuts? I'm nuts about you. I wish we didn't live so far away. But you can come on a visit to my place any time. If you don't mind being surrounded by all my stupid siblings. Or I can come and visit you??? Hint hint!

Love from Dan

P.S. It was truly great meeting you.

Honestly. He *is* nuts. If *only* he were older. And not so daft. And good looking.

'Who's it from then?' asks Anna, stirring soup at the stove. She tastes it delicately. 'More pepper, Eggs. Carefully.'

Eggs likes cooking. He even helps make Eggs Benedict, his namesake. Well, he's called Benedict, Anna's slightly poncey choice, but no-one's ever called him that. He started off as Baby Benny and for the last two years he's been Eggs. Possibly Pickled. Sometimes Scrambled. Often *Bad*.

'It's just some silly scribble from Dan,' I say, stuffing the letter into my pocket.

Anna raises her eyebrows. 'I *thought* you'd made a hit there.'

'For God's sake, Anna, he's only *twelve*. Don't be crazy.'

'I like that Dan. Oh, great, is he your boyfriend?' Eggs burbles, shaking pepper enthusiastically.

'Careful, Eggs. Just a *pinch*,' says Anna, catching hold of his wrist.

'Pinch pinch pinch,' Eggs giggles, pretending to pinch her arm.

'Idiot boy,' says Anna fondly, turning him upside down and tickling his exposed tummy.

'I'm going to do my homework,' I say.

I usually hang around the kitchen for a bit first but I don't particularly enjoy watching Anna and Eggs together. It always makes me feel weird. Like I was jealous or something. Not that I want to play about with Eggs in the slightest. And I certainly don't want Anna tickling me! She'd fall flat on her back if she tried to pick me up anyway. I weigh much more than her already, even though she's heaps taller.

Anna never tried any romping, tickling, cuddling mumsie stuff with me. I'm too old and she's too young. Of course there's far more of an age gap between Anna and Dad. He's nearly old enough to be *her* dad. He teaches Art and Anna was a student at his college. Dad didn't teach her. She did textiles. She used to work part time as a design consultant but that firm went bust so she's been looking for a new opening for ages. Dad still teaches at the college. The students haven't gone back yet but he's out at some college meeting nevertheless.

'Hang on a tick, Ellie,' says Anna. 'I don't know when your dad's going to get back. You know what he's like. But I'm supposed to be starting this Italian evening class tonight, so you wouldn't be an angel and put Eggs to bed for me?'

'Look, like I *said*, I've got all this homework,' I whine. For a while. And then I change tack and point out that other girls get paid for being a babysitter.

'Cheek! I'm not a *baby*,' Eggs intervenes. 'Why is it baby*sitter* anyway? They don't sit on the baby, do they?'

'Shut up, Eggs, or I'll take great delight in sitting on you,' I say.

I do agree in the end. Very very reluctantly. Though I can't see why Anna's making such a point of starting up this Italian evening class. It's not as if we're going to romp in Rome or flourish in Florence. We will get wet in Wales, as always.

She gets Eggs all bathed and ready for bed after supper, so all I'm supposed to do is supervise his last wee and stuff him into bed. Ha ha.

He starts capering about like a monkey and whenever I catch him he screams and giggles and squirms. When Dad comes in at last Eggs runs down the hall to him yelling at the top of his voice.

'Hey, hey! Why aren't you in bed, Mr Eggs-and-Bacon?' says Dad. He looks at me reproachfully. 'You shouldn't get him so excited before he goes to bed, Ellie, he'll be too worked up to sleep.'

Like it's *my* fault!!! That's the thanks I get. And it's dead annoying because Eggs does quieten down with Dad. He snuggles up on his lap and Dad reads him a Little Bear story. Eggs smiles angelically and

59

gently strokes each picture of Little Bear with his finger.

They're *my* Little Bear books actually. I can't ever remember Dad reading them to me. Not when I was all sleepy and snuggled up like that.

'What's up, Ellie?' Dad says suddenly. 'Are you sulking?'

'No, I'm *not* sulking. I'm just sitting here. There's no crime in that, is there?'

'*Read*, Dad,' Eggs insists. 'Don't talk to Smelly Ellie.'

'Eggs!' says Dad – but he chuckles.

Suddenly I can't stand either of them. It's suffocating even being in the same room as them. I stalk off to my bedroom and put on some music. Loud.

I suppose I ought to make a start on all this horrible homework but I catch sight of myself in the mirror and my hair looks awful, sort of exploding in all directions, so I have to brush it into submission and experiment with different hairstyles. I can scrunch it up into a little top-knot so it looks neater – almost OK – but then it makes my face look so much fatter. Oh, God, my face *is* fatter. It's like a huge great white beachball, and I'm getting a spot on my chin, and there's a little one on my nose too, a pink-and-white polka-dot beachball. I can't *stand* spots. Anna says I should never ever touch them but it's OK for her, she's got this incredible English rose skin, I don't think she's ever had a spot in her life.

I have a little squeezing session. It doesn't help. I feel so ugly. No wonder I haven't got a boyfriend.

No-one will ever want to go out with me. Apart from Dan. And he's so short-sighted even *he* would probably run away from me screaming if he polished up his specs and saw me properly.

I pick up his letter and read it again. Dad suddenly comes barging into my room.

'Dad! You're not supposed to come into my room without *knocking*!'

'I *did* knock. You just didn't hear me because of that awful row. Turn it *down*. I've just put Eggs to bed.'

Eggs Eggs Eggs Eggs Eggs. I see him as a row of Humpty Dumptys sitting on a wall. I tip them off one at a time, smash smash smash smash smash.

'Oh, of course, we mustn't disturb the boy wonder,' I say, switching off my CD player. 'OK? Happy now? Total silence so his little lordship can nod off in peace.'

'I didn't say you had to turn it off altogether,' says Dad. 'What's *up* with you, Ellie? You're so prickly all the time now.' He comes closer, tugging at his beard the way he always does when he's worried. 'Hey, what have you done to your face? It's bleeding.'

'I haven't done anything,' I say, covering my chin with my hand. 'Now would you mind leaving me alone so I can get on with my homework?'

'That's not homework. It's a letter. Who's it from, eh?'

'It's *my* letter, Dad,' I say, crumpling it up. Not quite quickly enough. He sees the end bit.

'Love from Dan! It's a love letter!' he says.

'No, it isn't!'

'So who on earth is this Dan? When did you get yourself a boyfriend, Ellie?'

'I haven't *got* a boyfriend! Will you just mind your own business, *please*,' I say, stuffing the stupid letter in my skirt pocket.

When Dad's gone I sigh deeply and put my head in my arms. I think about crying but actually fall asleep. I wake up with a stiff neck. I find I can't sleep when I go to bed.

Dad puts his head round the door when he comes upstairs to bed himself. 'Are you asleep, Ellie?' he whispers.

'Yes.'

'Anna told me about the boyfriend. He's that weird brainy kid in the anorak, right?'

'Wrong wrong wrong. He is *not* my boyfriend. Oh, God, I'm getting so sick of this,' I say, putting my head under the pillow.

'OK OK. Calm down. Sorry. Anna says I shouldn't tease you. Ellie?'

I stay underneath the pillow. There's a pause. Then I feel a slight pressure as he bends forward.

'Nightie nightie,' Dad whispers, kissing the pillow instead of me.

I wait. Then I whisper, 'Pyjama pyjama.' I take the pillow off my face. But Dad's gone out of the room already.

I still can't sleep. I hang on to the pillow for something to cuddle. I wish I'd kept some of my cuddly toys from when I was little. I had this blue elephant called Nellie and when I was Eggs's age I always had to lug her around with me. I talked to her constantly as if she were real, so you didn't just get me then, you got an Ellie-and-Nellie package.

I also had a panda called Bartholomew and a giraffe called Mabel and a big rag doll with orange hair called Marmalade.

I had really grown out of them all by the time Eggs was born, apart from Nellie. When Eggs started crawling he ignored all his own new cuddly toys and always wanted mine.

We once had a fight over Nellie. Eggs was screaming and screaming and wouldn't give her back. I could see it was a bit ridiculous a girl like me wrestling with a toddler over a dirty toy elephant with a wonky trunk – but I wouldn't give up. And then Eggs was suddenly sick all over Nellie. I insisted he'd done it on purpose. I said Nellie was spoilt for ever. My mother had made her for me when I was little. I bawled like a baby.

Anna sluiced Nellie down and put her in the washing machine. She ended up a rather naff pale mauve and her stuffing went lumpy. She was still Nellie but I insisted she was spoilt and I threw her in the dustbin.

I wish I hadn't. I wished it almost the minute the dustmen carted her off. I know it's totally mad but I still sometimes think of her now, lying amongst rotting Chinese takeaways and soggy teabags on some stinking rubbish tip, her trunk crumpled in despair.

I threw all my other toys out when I redecorated my room, wanting to change everything, to stop being that sad silly dreamy fat girl. I wanted to remodel a new shiny hip version of Ellie to match my new room. I painted it bright blue with red furniture and yellow curtains, primary colours for a very secondary style. I tried to be bright and snappy and cheerful to match but I couldn't keep it up. In fact right now I feel so dark and dreary and dismal I feel my matching habitat would be down a drain.

I clutch the pillow close. When I was younger I used to have Nadine sleep over at my house at least once a week. We'd never bother with campbeds and sleeping bags, we'd just snuggle up together in my bed. Nadine's not the cuddliest of girls, her elbows are sharp and she's very wriggly, but it was great fun all the same. We'd make up ghost stories so gross and gory that I'd have nightmares when we eventually got to sleep, but that was OK too because I could hang on to Nadine and feel the knobs on her spine as I cuddled up against her, her long hair tickling my face.

Only now Nadine has got Liam to cuddle. I still can't believe it even though I've met him now. I wonder how she got on with him on their walk. And Magda with Greg. Nadine and Liam, Magda and Greg, Ellie and no-one at all . . .

I drift off to sleep at long last. I dream. Ellie and Dan. Not the real Dan – the pretend boy, the one with blond hair and brown eyes. He waits for me outside school and we go off for a walk together down by the river. He holds my hand while we're walking along the street but when we get to the secluded riverside he pulls me close, his arms go round me, he whispers lovely things, he lifts my hair and kisses my neck, my ears, my mouth, we're kissing properly, it's so beautiful, we're lying on the mossy bank, entwined, I am his and he is mine and he whispers that he loves me, that he loved me from the moment we first set eyes on each other when he dodged round the parked car and we nearly collided, and I whisper that I love him too.

'I love you,' I whisper, and I wake up. I've never had such a vivid dream. I can still see the dappled sunlight on our skin, smell the honey musk of his chest, hear the beat of his heart, feel the warmth of his body . . .

That is where I am, where I want to stay. I'm a stranger in this banal world of bathroom and breakfast. I won't say a word as I sip coffee and spoon cornflakes. We sit at the table, Dad, Anna, Eggs and me. Four sides of the table, four members of a family, but they don't seem to have any connection with me whatsoever.

Dad is saying something to me but I'm not listening. It seems so strange that the only reason I'm sitting at this table is that the eight pints of blood in his body are similar to mine. He's just a plump middle-aged guy with an embarrassing haircut and beard way too old to wear that silly T-shirt. That small boy with the yelping laugh choking on his cornflakes has even less to do with me. The calm woman in her white shirt nothing at all.

She's saying something about me missing the bus if I'm not careful, and she's right. It's there at the stop when I'm only halfway down the road. I could try running, but I don't want my skirt to ride up even further, and besides, maybe I don't really *want* to catch the boring old bus. I can always walk to school. Just in case . . .

So I walk, past the bus stop, down the street, round the corner. The parked car's not there, he's not there either . . . YES HE IS! That's him, right down at the end. Walking towards me!

My dream is still so real it's as if I know him, as if we went for that walk together and were in each other's arms down by the river.

He's getting nearer, wearing a blue denim shirt today. It looks great with his colouring. He's looking straight ahead. Is he looking at me? Looking *for* me? What if he dreamt about me too? What if he somehow dreamt the very same dream?

I walk on and he walks on too. I can see his features now, his brown eyes, his straight nose, his sweet mouth, he's smiling, he's smiling at me. I shall smile too, a deeply significant smile to show that we share a secret . . .

'Hi,' he says, a few paces away.

Hi! To *me*? Is he really talking to me? He *can't* be. My head swivels to see if there's someone standing behind me. No-one. It's me. Oh, God, I feel such an idiot. I try to say Hi back but my throat is a sandy Sahara, so dry it comes out as a croak. Then he's past, he's walking on, I've lost it, I've lost my chance. He must think me a complete fool, only capable of frog-talk.

I am late for school again. Mrs Henderson gives me a detention. Another one. Two in two days. Mrs

Henderson suggests that I seem to be going for some sort of record.

'Not a wise move, Eleanor,' she adds threateningly.

I don't know what to do. I'm not fussed about old Hockeysticks Henderson. It's me. I think I'm really going mad. Because now I'm in school and I'm breathing in the familiar smell of rubber trainers and canteen chip fat and Body Shop scent and Clearasil my dream is fading fast. I was starting to *believe* the dream was real, that the blond boy and I were really involved.

I've got to stop this fast. I've got to tell Nadine and Magda that I made it all up.

But I still don't get a word in edgeways, not even at lunchtime on our steps. Nadine goes on about Liam, Liam, Liam. She's inked a whole series of lovehearts all the way up her arm. She'll give herself blood poisoning if she's not careful. It's as if she's dyed her brain with his name too, because he's all she can talk about. Not that *they* seem to talk at all. He's barely said anything to her so far. They just skive off and snog, basically. Which is a little *too* basic, if you ask me.

'Well, I didn't ask you,' Nadine snaps.

Magda says that Greg does too much talking, he never stops. He showed her how to work out the Maths homework although she already knew perfectly well how to do it. And then he started giving her tips on Science into the bargain.

'How about a few tips on Human Biology?' Magda suggested on their way home.

But he was too thick to take up her offer. He might be dead brainy but he's brain-dead when it come to physical relationships, obviously.

'It's not necessarily obvious,' Magda retorts. 'I've just got to give him time. Redheads are *known* for their tempestuous natures.'

'You're ever so picky about Liam and Greg,' says Nadine. 'What's bugging you, eh, Ellie?'

'Nothing's bugging me.'

'You're not feeling just the teeniest bit left out?' says Nadine.

'Certainly not!'

'Well, she's probably fed up because her Dan is so far away and she can't see him,' says Magda.

'If he even exists,' says Nadine, staring at me very intently.

I feel my heart pounding underneath my blouse. Nadine knows me so well. I hate the way her green eyes are gleaming.

'Oh yes, he's a figment of my imagination,' I say, staring at them both. I pause. Then I feel in my skirt pocket and produce my crumpled letter. 'A figment of my imagination who somehow miraculously has managed to write to me,' I say, flashing the letter in their faces.

I cover up most of the words but I show them the important part: *Love from Dan.*

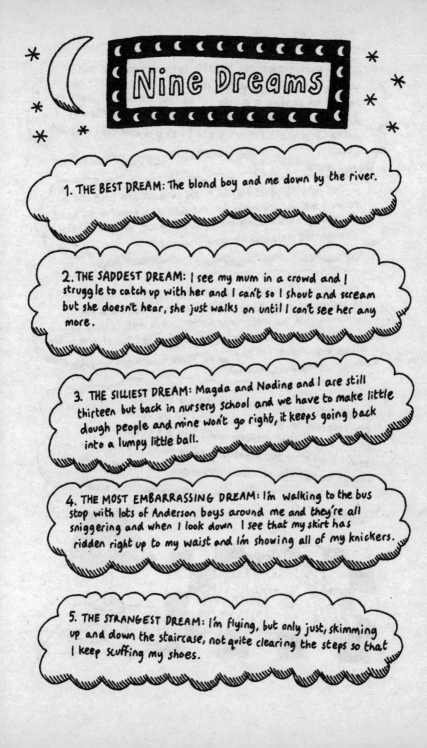

Nine Dreams

1. THE BEST DREAM: The blond boy and me down by the river.

2. THE SADDEST DREAM: I see my mum in a crowd and I struggle to catch up with her and I can't so I shout and scream but she doesn't hear, she just walks on until I can't see her any more.

3. THE SILLIEST DREAM: Magda and Nadine and I are still thirteen but back in nursery school and we have to make little dough people and mine won't go right, it keeps going back into a lumpy little ball.

4. THE MOST EMBARRASSING DREAM: I'm walking to the bus stop with lots of Anderson boys around me and they're all sniggering and when I look down I see that my skirt has ridden right up to my waist and I'm showing all of my knickers.

5. THE STRANGEST DREAM: I'm flying, but only just, skimming up and down the staircase, not quite clearing the steps so that I keep scuffing my shoes.

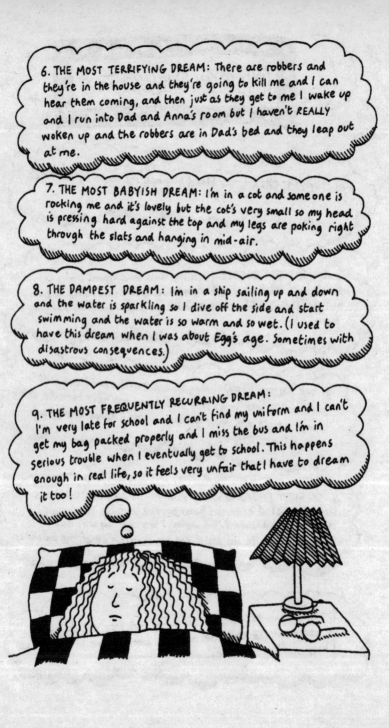

6. THE MOST TERRIFYING DREAM: There are robbers and they're in the house and they're going to kill me and I can hear them coming, and then just as they get to me I wake up and I run into Dad and Anna's room but I haven't REALLY woken up and the robbers are in Dad's bed and they leap out at me.

7. THE MOST BABYISH DREAM: I'm in a cot and someone is rocking me and it's lovely but the cot's very small so my head is pressing hard against the top and my legs are poking right through the slats and hanging in mid-air.

8. THE DAMPEST DREAM: I'm in a ship sailing up and down and the water is sparkling so I dive off the side and start swimming and the water is so warm and so wet. (I used to have this dream when I was about Egg's age. Sometimes with disastrous consequences.)

9. THE MOST FREQUENTLY RECURRING DREAM: I'm very late for school and I can't find my uniform and I can't get my bag packed properly and I miss the bus and I'm in serious trouble when I eventually get to school. This happens enough in real life, so it feels very unfair that I have to dream it too!

Five Alive

(but only just, and all dying of embarrassment and boredom!)

There's no way I can ever tell the truth now. So I'm stuck. Treading in treacle, superglued into silence.

I write back to Dan. Mostly because I need him to write back to me again so I can show off his letter to Nadine and Magda. Which is so mean.

He writes back. And I write back. And he writes back. And so it goes on. They're just silly letters. He goes on about school and stuff and things he's reading and he tells a lot of corny old jokes. He puts 'Love from Dan' at the end each time, but they're not *love* letters.

Dad says we're like Elizabeth Barrett and Robert Browning and sniggers. They are dead poets. I mutter something ultra-unpoetical along the lines that I wish Dad were dead too. Dad hears and gets narked and says I've completely lost my sense of humour. Anna surprisingly takes my side. She says Dad's crass and insensitive and she's sick of it, so goodness knows how Ellie feels. Both Dad and I blink at her a bit. She doesn't usually rush to my defence. I think maybe she and Dad have had a row. I heard a lot of angry whispers last night after Anna got back from her evening class. I don't know what's going on with them. I don't know what's going on with *me*.

I haven't even seen the dream Dan again. I caught the bus for a bit because Mrs Henderson was giving me so many detentions it was getting like I'd be stuck at school for a full twenty-four hours. But I chance walking today. I even hang around a second on the street where we met. Longer than a second actually. More like fifteen minutes. And I still don't get to see him. *And* I get another detention.

It's quite companionable actually because Nadine is doing a detention too. It's just the two of us. Mrs Henderson makes us write out *lines*, would you believe? I had to write out: I MUST PULL MYSELF TOGETHER AND TRY TO BE ON TIME.

I write it one hundred times. I don't feel pulled together. I feel as if I'm flying apart. And I tried to be on time to see Dream Dan. I couldn't try any harder if I wrote it out one million times.

Nadine's line is shorter than mine so even though she writes in an elaborate twirly way she still gets finished first. One hundred times: I MUST NOT BE INSOLANT.

She came to school with this amazing love-bite on her neck, a big blotch that looked impressively purple on her white skin.

'For God's sake, your Liam must have a mouth like a vacuum cleaner,' said Magda.

'Well, Nadine's always had a thing about vampires,' I said, trying to sound funny and flippant.

I couldn't stop staring at Nadine's love-bite. When we were little we used to experiment, sucking on each other's arms to see what it felt like. When we got older we agreed love-bites were *gross*. And yet now Nadine had one right at the front of her neck so that it wasn't even hidden by her hair. I tried not to think of Liam doing it to her but I couldn't help it. It made me feel so weird. I couldn't work out which I felt most, disgusted or envious.

Mrs Henderson's feelings were more straight-forward. 'I think you need to go to the medical cupboard for a sticky plaster, Nadine,' she said coldly. 'I don't want to look at that stupid mark on your neck. Surely you realize how silly it is to let someone do that to you. It's not exactly treating you with respect, is it? Let alone risking serious infection.'

Nadine scowled. 'Bet you're just jealous,' she muttered.

Not quietly enough. She got her detention too.

Mrs Henderson leaves us to finish our lines while she goes off to supervise a hockey practice.

'Well, I've done my stupid lines so I don't see why I can't go now,' says Nadine, fidgeting.

'She said we had to wait till she came back.'

'It's ridiculous. She's got no right to comment on what I do out of school hours,' says Nadine, fingering the plaster covering her bite.

'What on earth did your mum and dad say when they saw it?

'Don't be mad! I wound this scarf right round my neck, right? I tell you, if they found out about Liam they'd go seriously bananas.'

'Nadine?'

'What?' She doesn't bother to look up. She gets a magazine out of her schoolbag and starts flipping through the pages.

Nadine used to despise teen mags. She just read weird fanzines about her favourite bands and horror stories. But now she's reading this problem page as if her life depends on it.

'What's it feel like? You know – the love-bite?'

Nadine shrugs.

'Did you want him to do it?'

'Well, he wants to do a lot *more*.'

'And . . . do you let him?'

Nadine wriggles. 'Well, *some* things.' She hesitates. 'Look, keep this a secret, right? Don't even tell Magda.' There's no-one else in the room but she still leans forward and then whispers.

'Nadine!' I say, stunned.

'Well, what's wrong with that, eh?' says Nadine. 'Honestly, Ellie, you're such a baby.'

'No, I'm not.'

'Everyone does that with their boyfriends.'

'Do they?'

'Well, I take it you don't do it with Dan.' Nadine looks at me sharply.

I try to imagine such intimacy with both my Dans. I think of doing it with the dream Dan and the blood starts beating in my own neck. Then I think of doing it with the real Dan and I practically crack up laughing.

'What are you grinning about?' says Nadine. 'So you *did* fool around with your Dan.'

We'd certainly make fools of ourselves! 'Chance would be a fine thing,' I mutter. 'We don't see each other, do we?'

Dan (real, of course) has been nagging me to go and stay with him or invite him down to London. I keep putting him off with elaborate excuses, but it's getting a bit awkward. The whole situation is so difficult I let out this long sigh.

'Do you really miss him, Ellie?' says Nadine softly. She puts her arm round me, crumpling her magazine.

I snuggle into her, though I feel guilty. 'It's just . . . Oh, I wish I could explain properly, Nad,' I whisper.

'I know,' says Nadine – though she doesn't. 'Look, things are a bit difficult with Liam and me too. We had this sort of row yesterday.'

'Yeah?'

'Because I won't, you know, go the whole way. I just don't feel ready to. And the magazines say you shouldn't do it till you *are* ready – look.' She reaches for the magazine and shows me this letter.

'Bla bla bla, "so don't let your boyfriend do . . ."

Ooh! "And if he complains that his tackle . . ."
What's his *tackle*? Like in *fishing rod*?'

We both get a fit of the giggles.

'No, you nutcase. It's his . . . *you* know.'

Oh. Yes. Even *I* can work it out now. I carry on
reading the letter. 'So does your Liam get all narked
with you like the guy in the letter?'

'He did yesterday. He said he'd been ever so
patient. And didn't I love him enough. And I said I
loved him desperately but I still didn't feel ready,
right? And he said if I wasn't ready now I never
would be, and what was the matter with me, didn't
I want our relationship to develop.' Nadine's not
giggling now, she's nearly in tears.

'Oh, Nad. He's acting like a right . . . *tackle*!' I
hope she'll laugh, but a tear drips down her cheek.

'No, I can understand, Ellie. I mean, it's so
frustrating for him—'

'That's *rubbish*! Look, you don't have to do
anything with him. You're only thirteen, for goodness' sake. It's against the *law*.'

'Yes, but nobody takes any notice of that. And all
his other girlfriends have always done it, no bother.'

'There you are! You don't want to be one of a
whole long *line* of stupid girls. Honestly, Nadine,
where's your *brain*?'

'I have often been tempted to ask that question
myself,' says Mrs Henderson, walking through the
door.

Nadine shoves her mag under her desk and bends
her head so that her hair hides her tear-stained face.

Mrs Henderson approaches. She's actually

looking *concerned*. 'What's up, mmm?' she says, in a different sort of voice altogether. 'I know you girls think I come from another planet – but maybe I can still help. What's the problem?'

Nadine fidgets behind her hair. I look down at my lap.

'Nadine?' says Mrs Henderson. 'Are you upset about a boyfriend, is that it?'

I suppose it's a reasonably obvious guess, with Nadine's neck still purple.

Nadine keeps quiet.

'It does help to talk things over, you know,' says Mrs Henderson. 'And no problem is unique. I'm sure I've had similar problems myself.'

I immediately get this amazing image in my head of Mrs Henderson doing this particular thing to Mr Henderson. I have to bite the sides of my cheeks to stop myself shrieking with laughter. Nadine's shoulders shake. She's obviously got the same mental image. Thank God Mrs Henderson doesn't twig the trouble.

'Don't cry, Nadine,' she says gently.

Nadine gives a little gasp.

Mrs Henderson interprets it as a sob. 'Oh, come on, now. Well, I can't force you to confide in me. But don't forget, I'm always here. Now. How far have you got with your lines?'

Nadine hands her page over, her head still bent.

'"I must not be insolant." One hundred times. Oh dear, I really ought to give you another hundred: "I must learn to spell:" In-so-*lent*, Nadine. But never mind. Off you go now. And you too, Eleanor.'

I hand in my own page, hoping she won't count the lines as I'm still only at seventy-something. She scans them quickly, raises an eyebrow, but waves me away.

Nadine and I hold our breath till we're safely down the corridor, and then we let out great *whoops* of laughter. At least it cheers Nadine up for a bit. But she still can't seem to see any kind of sense at all.

The next day I have a private word with Magda.

'She's totally mental,' says Magda.

'I know. But there's no way I can get through to her,' I say.

'I'll have a go,' says Magda.

'Well. Do be ever so tactful. And don't let out that *I* said anything, eh?' I say, but Magda isn't listening to me.

'Nadine! Come over here! Ellie says you're going to do it with Liam, you silly cow.'

Practically every girl in the playground looks up and gawps.

'Magda! You and your big mouth!' I say.

'I think it's you and *your* big mouth, Ellie,' says Nadine. 'Thanks a bunch.'

'Hey, don't be like that,' says Magda, rushing over to her and putting her arm round her neck.

'Get off me, Magda!'

'I just want to talk to you, Nadine.'

'Yeah, but I don't *want* to talk about it, OK?'

'We're mates, aren't we?'

'But this isn't about you and me and Ellie. It's just to do with me and Liam. So you keep your nose out of it, OK? And you too, Ellie,' says Nadine, and she stalks off by herself.

'Shall we go after her?' says Magda.

'We'll be wasting our time,' I say miserably.

I know Nadine too well. She'll never listen to either of us now. I feel I've really blown it. I've betrayed Nadine's confidence – and I haven't helped her in the slightest.

She barely talks to either of us all day. When school is over she goes rushing off to meet up with Liam, who's waiting for her by the wall.

'So let's have a word with him, eh?' says Magda.

'No! You can't! And Nadine would kill us,' I say.

We don't get the chance anyway, because Nadine and Liam hurry away. It's cold, so Liam is wearing this incredible black leather jacket.

'That is a seriously sexy jacket,' Magda says wistfully. 'He might be a pig but he sure looks good. Why can't Greg wear a leather jacket? He's got this naff zippy thing that is practically an anorak.'

'How's it going with Greg, anyway?' I ask.

'Well . . .' says Magda, and sighs.

'*He* doesn't want you to . . .?'

'Per-lease!' says Magda. 'Greg??? No, he's OK, he's quite sweet actually, but all we seem to do is talk homework and hang out at McDonald's. Ah! Which reminds me. One of Greg's mates, Adam, is having a party this Saturday. His parents are away for the weekend so they're planning a serious rave-up. Want to come?'

I stare at her, heart beating.

She mistakes my hesitation. 'Look, I know you

and Dan are an item and the last thing you want is to meet someone new at a party. I mean, you've *got* a boyfriend.'

Oh, Magda! If you only knew. A party. I've never ever been to a party before. Well, of course I've been to *parties* – the little-girly balloons-and-birthday-cake kind. But I've never been to a party with *boys*.

'Please come, Ellie. It should be a laugh, if nothing else. Maybe *I'll* meet a new boyfriend. Greg is OK, but he's seriously lacking when it comes to street cred. His mates might have more potential.'

I don't know what to say, what to do. A serious rave-up. No parents. And boys, boys, boys.

It sounds incredible.

It sounds incredibly scary. I think drink. I think drugs. I think bedrooms.

I want to go. Maybe I'll meet a *real* boyfriend. One of Greg's mates. Although perhaps they'll have girls already.

'Are you sure it won't be just a couple party?' I say.

'*No*, that's the point. This Adam is inviting along half Year Eleven at Andersons, and most of them are totally *un*coupled. They're desperate for more girls. Greg practically begged me to ask some along. I was thinking – who else shall we ask, eh?'

There doesn't seem much point in asking Nadine. Magda asks Chrissie, but she's already going to a party that night. She asks Jess but she says it's not her kind of thing, thanks. She asks Amna who says she'd give anything to go but her dad would go bananas.

'Maybe *my* dad won't let me,' I mumble.

'Rubbish. Your dad seems really cool to me,' says Magda.

Dad always makes a fuss of Magda when she comes round to our house.

'I'll ask him for you if you like,' says Magda. 'OK?'

I don't really want her to. I don't know if I really want to go to this party. What will I wear? What will I say? What am I expected to *do*?'

'What's up?' says Magda. 'He knows you're going out with Dan so you won't let any other boy try it on at the party – so he can't object, can he?'

Oh help. I'll have to keep Magda away from Dad at all costs. Dad thinks it hilariously funny that I write so much to the real Dan. He'll talk about him to Magda and she'll twig what he's *really* like.

'No, leave Dad to me, I'll handle him,' I say firmly. 'OK, I'll go to the party with you, Magda.'

'You won't regret it, I promise,' says Magda.

I regret agreeing almost immediately. I tell Dad about the party, practically hoping he'll say no way. Anna is very doubtful, and asks straight away if the parents are going to be there and what about the drink/drugs situation and suppose there are gate-crashers?

'Look, I don't want to be rude, but I wasn't asking you, Anna, I was asking Dad,' I say. Though I'm secretly glad she's pointed out all these objections.

I hope Dad will take them all on board and agree it's out of the question.

But he doesn't. 'Come off it, Anna, you're sounding positively middle-aged,' he says. 'This is just some tame little party at a schoolboy's house. Why shouldn't Ellie go? And she'll be fine if Magda's going too. That kid knows what she's doing all right.'

'I don't give a damn about Magda. It's Ellie. Does she know what *she's* doing?' says Anna.

'We've got to credit her with some sense. You know enough not to do anything stupid, right, Ellie? You go to your party and have fun.'

'I don't think you're being a very responsible parent,' says Anna. 'But then you're not famed for your responsibility, are you?'

'What's that supposed to mean?' says Dad.

'I think you know,' says Anna.

'I don't have a clue,' says Dad.

I don't have a clue either but I leave them to have a row while I go up to my room. I get out all my clothes and try on every single item. I look a mess in everything. Fat. Babyish. So utterly uncool that I despair.

I'm still despairing on Saturday evening, even though Magda arrives early and gives me advice.

'Dress down. You'll look as if you're trying too hard if you dress up. Wear your jeans. *Not* the cruddy ripped ones. The black.'

OK. So that's my black jeans, even though they're so tight I shall be cut in two if I sit down.

'You won't be sitting down, babe. You'll be dancing,' says Magda. She looks at my boots. 'Well, lumbering.' She sees my face. '*Joke*, Ellie!'

I don't feel like laughing. I feel so fat I select my biggest baggiest T-shirt to wear with the jeans.

'No no no,' says Magda. 'Dress down but also dress sexy.'

'But I'm not.'

'You don't have to *be* it. Just look it. Something little and tight on top. For God's sake, Ellie, yours are Wonders *without* the bra. So if you've got it, flaunt it.'

I've never felt less like flaunting in my entire life. But I do as I'm told and put on an old purple T-shirt I wore when I was practically a little kid. It strains across my embarrassing chest. I look as if I'm wearing a giant rubber band but Magda insists I look fine. She makes me up with purple shadowed eyes to match the T-shirt and fusses that we haven't got deep purple nail varnish too.

Dad is giving us a lift to this Adam's house. (Magda is meeting Greg there.) Dad winks approvingly at Magda, who is looking ultra-cute in a little black skirt and a black-and-white top so short she shows her tiny waist whenever she moves. Dad stops winking and blinks when he sees me. 'Ellie!' he says.

'What?' I say, trying to sound surly and defiant – but my voice cracks.

'Mmm. Well. You look very . . .' He looks over at Anna. 'Maybe this party isn't such a good idea after all,' he says. 'I didn't realize it was going to be so . . . grown up.'

Anna raises her eyebrows. Eggs jumps up onto the armchair. 'Look at me! See how tall I am! I'm a grown-up. I want to go to the party.' He jumps up onto the arm and slips.

Anna is kept busy quelling his yells and rubbing his sore bits. Dad sighs and offers us an arm each. 'Allow me to escort you, ladies,' he says.

He fusses in the car, grilling Magda about Greg and the other boys. He asks all Anna's questions about parents and drink and drugs and insists that he will be waiting outside at twelve to take us home.

'Like Cinderella. Only ball gowns aren't what they used to be,' he says, giving my T-shirt another nervous glance.

He looks a little reassured when we draw up outside Adam's house, one of those cosy mock-Tudor jobs with a little goldfish pond and a garden gnome in a little red plaster cap and matching bootees. There's a car parked in the drive.

'Ah. At least his parents *are* at home,' says Dad.

'Cool subterfuge,' Magda breathes in my ear.

But guess what? It's not subterfuge at all. Adam's mum comes to the door, in a pastel sweater and leggings, holding one of those big plastic plates with little sections for nuts and crisps and twiglets. 'Ah! You two are . . .?'

'I'm Magda and she's Ellie,' says Magda faintly.

'And you're friends of Adam's?'

'Well, I'm a friend of Greg. And he's a friend of Adam,' says Magda. 'And Ellie's *my* friend.'

I don't *feel* like being Magda's friend, not after tonight!

This is not a rave-up. This is a terrible embarrassing non-event. Adam is a boy who looks almost as young as Dan even though he's in Year Eleven. He's a little weedy whatsit with an extremely protruberant Adam's apple (appropriate), which bobs up and down when he talks.

For a long terrible while it's just Adam and Magda and me in the living room, with Adam's mum bustling in and out offering us party nibbles and some ghastly punch that's got about one tot of red wine to every gallon of fruit juice. Damp shreds of maraschino cherry and tinned mandarin lodge against my teeth whenever I try to take a drink.

Adam hisses that his parents decided against their weekend break because his dad has a shocking cold. We hear frequent explosive sneezing from upstairs. I don't think there are going to be any heavy bedroom sessions tonight somehow.

Greg turns up eventually. Magda gives him a hard time, whispering furiously in his crimson ear.

One more boy arrives half an hour later. He's clutching a can of lager and boasts that he's had a few already. He keeps belching. Adam finds this funny and swigs from the can too when his mum is out of the room.

I would sooner go out with Dan than these two.

I would sooner go out with *Eggs*.

Why doesn't anyone else come???

After endless awful ages there's another knock and it sounds as if there's a whole crowd of boys outside but when Adam's mum goes to the door there's a whole load of spluttering and mumbled excuses and someone says they've come to the wrong house and they all charge off.

So we are left. Five of us. We are the party. And

I don't drink and I don't take drugs and I don't dance and I don't go up to a bedroom with a boy. I don't even *talk* to a boy.

I just sit there at the first and worst party of my life.

Nine Parties

1. IDEAL 'I WISH' PARTY: just me and Dream Dan...

2. MY BEST LITTLE-GIRLY PARTY: when my mum was still alive and she fixed a rainbow party with red strawberries and orange juice and yellow bananas and green jelly and blue-iced birthday cake and indigo blueberry crème brûlée and violet cream chocolates and there were rainbow balloons and she hung crystals up at the windows so there were rainbows all over the room when the sun shone.

3. MY BEST BIG-GIRL PARTY: my twelfth birthday when I had an ice-cream party with all different varieties, and ice-cream soda and a big ice-cream birthday cake.

4. NADINE'S BEST PARTY: when I stayed over on her birthday night when we were little kids and we played Vampire Barbie and smeared red Smartie dye all over our Barbies' mouths and made them manically attack all baby Natasha's fluffy toys.

5. MAGDA'S BEST PARTY: when her mum and dad took us all to Planet Hollywood and then to a Brad Pitt movie.

6. FUNNIEST PARTY: Eggs's Christening party, when he wouldn't stop screaming and Dad said, 'Let ME hold him,' and he patted Eggs on the back and Eggs was amazingly, copiously sick all down Dad's posh suit.

7. WETTEST PARTY: the picnic party in Wales when it drizzled most of the time, and then positively tipped down in stair-rods. Dopey Dan looks even less fetching with his anorak hood up!

8. NEXT-TO-WORST PARTY: my birthday party just after Dad and Anna got together and I kept arguing about the games and hated the birthday cake even though Anna had made it in a special blue elephant shape and I started flicking bits of it about and got told off and I complained and then I cried in front of everyone.

9. WORST PARTY: Adam's party!

Six Letters

Dear Dan,

    I went to a great party on Saturday night. A real rave-up.

    I danced.

    I drank.

    I socialized.

    I didn't get home till dawn.

Dear Dan,

    I am a liar. You should see my tongue. We always used to say when we were little that you got black spots on your tongue if you told a lie. Mine is black as coal all over. It was a truly terrible party if you really want to know. So mind-boggingly awful that I phoned my dad to come and get me early.

    I felt so STUPID. There are all these long

89

fussing articles in the papers about the teenagers of today and how they're all into drink and drugs and snogging everything in sight. Well, I am leading the most dull dreary demure life imaginable. And it's dead boring.

I feel sort of OUT of things. Like I don't belong anywhere. Do you ever get that feeling? Of course you don't. You're a boy, you obviously don't know what it's like. You don't ever have to worry about how you look and what you wear and whether you're popular.

I don't know why I'm writing all this rubbish. It's just it's late at night and I can't sleep and I'm feeling so fed up and there's no-one I can really talk to, so hard luck, Dan, I'm rabbiting on to you. I've always had my two best friends, Magda and Nadine, to talk to - but it's sort of different now. I'm still friends with Magda but she's such a jokey lively fun sort of girl she doesn't always understand if I'm feeling depressed. And she's got this boyfriend Greg who she's seeing quite a lot of. She's not THAT keen on him — but he's OK. They were at this awful party but it was all right for them because they could just sit in a corner by themselves and snog. Magda initiated the embrace. She just pounced and Greg was powerless. But he didn't seem to mind. Well, he wouldn't. Magda is a pretty stunning girl.

Usually if I'm feeling low I confide in my other friend Nadine, who is a naturally gloomy sort of girl. Nadine and I have been best friends ever since we were tiny tots. We even used to dress alike and pretend we were twins (which was a little dopey as I've always been small and round with frizzy hair and Nadine is tall and thin with dead-straight hair, but we never let that deter us.) But now... she's got this boyfriend Liam and he's much older and Nadine thinks he's so cool and yet I think he's a creep because of the way he treats her, expecting her to do all sorts of stuff — well, YOU know — and Nadine told me all this and I told Magda and Magda told Nadine she was an idiot and Nadine stopped talking to us and she still won't make it up and I'm dead worried about her. And I'm worried about my dad and my stepmother because right this minute they're having an argument in their bedroom. I can hear them even though they're whispering. I don't know why they're having all these rows. They used to get on so well together. In fact when Anna first came to live with us I used to hope they WOULD fight, I used to do my best to wind Anna up and kept telling tales on her to Dad. Not because I absolutely hated her. In fact, she's OK, really. Well, most of the time. But she's my stepmother and I never wanted any kind of substitute mum, because mine was the best in the world.

I'm not going to write about my mum because it might make me cry. ANYWAY, I've sort of got used to Anna now, it's like we're friends. Not GREAT friends, just OK, ordinary friends. She's always been so calm and quiet and happy which is just as well because I can get ever so stroppy and moody sometimes and my little brother Eggs is a right pain most of the time as you know only too well and my dad is the worst of us all for going ballistic but Anna's always known how to handle him, she's always calmed him down. It's always been like he's this great growly dog and she knows just the way to give him a firm word and then a pat so he drools all over her like a puppy. But she's lost the trick now. Or maybe she's got fed up playing that game, I don't know. She seems to want to be her own person more, especially now Eggs has started school. She's tried to get back into doing design work, only there aren't any jobs going at the moment, which is a bit depressing for her, and then she started this evening class and last Tuesday there was a great ding-dong because I was going round to Magda's and Dad had promised to be home to look after Eggs so Anna could go to the class only something cropped up at my dad's college and he didn't get back in time and Anna couldn't go to her class and when I got back I could see Anna had been crying. I can't see why going to this evening class should matter so much to her. It's Italian conversation and we're never ever going to GO to Italy, just boring old wet Wales. (Do you REALLY like it???) Mind you, I'd give anything to go to Italy because I want to see all the Art, and Magda says the ice-creams are mega-fantastic. And Italian guys are meant to be the sexiest guys in the world. I suppose Anna likes Art because she did go to Art School but she won't touch ice-creams, she's far too fussed about keeping her figure. And Anna isn't into sexy Italian guys because she's got Dad. Unless...

Oh, God, I've suddenly thought of something. Maybe Anna's got another bloke. A sexy Italian. Or is she just using the evening class as an excuse, and she's off meeting some mystery boyfriend somewhere? I've always wondered what on earth she sees in my dad as he's so much older than her, and she's pretty stunning to look at, and Dad's got this pot belly though he sucks in his stomach whenever he looks in the mirror and insists all his flab is solid muscle, and he wears jeans and denim jackets like he's young only he isn't, and then there's his awful beard and his long hair and those terrible sandals he wears in the summer. And it's not as if he's got the easiest personality—

I'll say! Dad just got up to go to the bathroom and he spotted my light on and he said, What on earth are you up to, Ellie? and he's switched my light off so I expect my writing's going up and down all over the place and you won't be able to read a thing but anyway it doesn't really matter because I don't think I'll be sending you this letter anyway as it's just a load of rambling rubbish and you'll think I've gone completely nuts.

Love, Ellie

Dear Ellie

You're not nuts at all. I'm so glad you sent your letter. It was the best letter I've ever had. It was as if I've seen through a little window right into your head. I've read it over and over. I carry it about with me. Well hidden, naturally.

I was just so amazed and bowled over to realize you can get so bothered and fed up and stuff. Me too, me too, me too! You are entirely WRONG about boys not knowing what it's like, though. I don't EVER feel like I belong anywhere. I feel as if I've been zapped here from my own special Planet Dan and now I'm plodding around totally alien territory and all the Earthlings are laughing at me. Absolutely wetting themselves. And even more now, because I'm reacting to alien air by erupting into loathsome pimples all over the place, yuck yuck yuck, and even though I anoint my spots with all sorts of junk Mum buys in Boots it doesn't help much. My entire body seems to be going berserk. I am not going into details but girls have NO IDEA AT ALL how embarrassing it can be. I wish I could hide inside a special spaceman suit with a fishbowl helmet and not have to make contact with anyone else ever. Except you.

You wrote 'Love Ellie' for the first time. That's the best bit of your letter. I've read those two tiny words over and over, so many times it's a wonder the ink hasn't worn right off the page, such is the ardour of my laser-gaze.

LOTS of love,
Dan XXX

Dear Dan,

I didn't mean to post that last letter! I just shoved it in an envelope in a tearing rush in the morning and put it in the letter box as I ran for school and THEN I remembered some of the stuff I'd said and I was so embarrassed. I even ran back to the letterbox and tried to wriggle my hand through the slot. Then this police panda car slowed down and I thought, Oh, my God, I'm going to get arrested for attempting to steal the Royal Mail. I wriggled my wrist free and sort of grinned sheepishly at these police guys and they just laughed at me.

MOST people laugh at me. I like the idea of wearing a spacesuit. I'd like one too. Only how can one communicate in a fishbowl helmet? You couldn't go shopping unless you did some serious miming to show you wanted the latest indie album, leaping in the air in manic mode. Come to think of it, you wouldn't be able to HEAR it. And what about talking to your friends? (Though one of my best friends still isn't talking to ME.) And school??? Though I'm not a brainbox like you obviously are, so I don't do much communicating with the teachers at the best of times.

This is the WORST of times. I feel seriously fed up. Oh, God, I'd better stop now or I'll write ANOTHER long rambly rubbishy letter. I didn't really put 'Love Ellie' last time, did I? I don't remember. I don't ever put Love to anyone, not even Luv or Lurve. I just put me.
                                                    Ellie.

Dear Ellie,
        You did SO put 'Love Ellie'. I have your letter here, beneath my heart. Well, that sounds poetic but it's not anatomically accurate. I don't have any pockets up at chest level. I've got your letter in my trouser pocket. So your words of Love (not Luv, not Lurve, LOVE) are actually rubbing against my thigh, only that sounds embarrassingly intimate and I don't want this letter to develop into one of those porny pervy jobs some of the guys at my school write to girls. No, their letters are probably not TO girls, they're just ABOUT girls.
        I don't want to think of you like that, Ellie. Not that you aren't absolutely wonderfully

96

attractive etc, etc, etc. It was love at first sight like I said. I knew you were the girl for me. I think about you all the time. I've never been in love before. I suppose I love my mum and dad (though they do go ON a bit, and act all silent and reproachful if I want to do anything normal like watch RED DWARF or BOTTOM or play computer games or go to a football match - because they just want to read books and listen to classical music and wear Oxfam and recycle everything and lead a life as Green as Grass they think I should too). I love my brothers and sisters a bit too (though like your brother Eggs they are Right Pains - no, Excruciating Agonies, especially when they come barging into my bedroom and read all my private stuff and mock my new hairstyle). I am trying to turn myself into a dead cool guy so you will look at me and decide you'll follow me, your lord, throughout the world. I haven't suddenly gone nuts - well, nuttier than I am already - it's something Juliet says. Are you doing ROMEO AND JULIET too? It's quite good though it's murder doing it at my school because we're all boys so some poor sap has to be Juliet when we read aloud. I was the original poor sap actually, and everyone fell about and I could see this was NOT going to improve my street cred among the lads so I had to camp it up and do Juliet in a silly high-pitched girly voice

97

which got me into trouble with the teacher -
shame, as he's quite a decent bloke really and
he's lent me some of his books - but it made
everyone think I'm a nut instead of a nerd,
only I don't want to be, and there's nothing I
can do about my weedy physique or lousy
complexion and I can't even earn any hard cash
for cool clothes till I'm fourteen BUT I did
think a haircut might help. Mum normally just
chops bits off here and there. NOT a pretty
sight. So I badgered her to let me go to a
proper barber and I said I wanted a radical
new hairstyle, one that would last. Until I see
you: WHEN WILL THAT BE??? You can come
and stay for the weekend any time but our
house is ever so crowded with kids' stuff. All
the flannels in our bathroom are currently
growing mustard and cress and you can't eat
off the table in the living room because it's
covered with a giant jigsaw puzzle and there
are ducks swimming in the bath (generally just
the plastic variety but you never know!) and if
you sleep in the only spare bed that means my
sisters Rhianne and Lara will be in the bunk
bed opposite and Rhianne sings all the time,
even when she's asleep, and Lara climbs into
bed with you at four in the morning, bringing
her entire soft toy menagerie with her. So you
would be ever so E.VE.R SO welcome but not
extremely comfortable. So how about if I stay
with you? I have this cousin who is going out
with a girl at London University so he drives

down most Friday nights and says he doesn't
mind giving me a lift, which is brilliant. So what
about next weekend? Although maybe I ought
to wear a space helmet for real. Made of
black ambulance glass. Because the new haircut
might just be a bit of a mistake. My mum
shook her head and sighed deeply when she saw
me. My dad got all worried that I'd joined
some skin-head gang. My brothers and sisters
fell about laughing. Which was NOTHING
compared to the reaction of the guys at
school. I am certainly well established as a nut
now. You will also get a right laugh when you
see me, Ellie. So... next week, yes? I'll be
arriving between eight and nine, depending on
traffic. See you S-O-O-O-O-N!

Lots and lots and lots of love,
Dan

Dear Dan,
    No, don't come next weekend! I'm sorry,
but it's Magda's birthday, and we're hanging out
there Saturday and then will be going out
celebrating somewhere, but it's girls only, I'm
afraid, so I can't ask you to come. In actual
fact I don't really think it would be a good idea
if you came at all because our spare bed
situation is pretty chronic too. (Eggs broke the
springs on the guest bed so it's just a camp
bed, the sort that suddenly springs shut when
you're inside it), so let's wait until we meet up
again in Wales, right? Do you go there at

Christmas? We do, it's completely crackers, we all have to wear six jumpers and it snows and there's frost INSIDE the windows, let alone outside, but it's becoming a loopy family tradition, worst luck. Still, if you're there too we could play Sir Edmund Hillary and Sherpa Tensing.

L. Ellie

Dear Ellie,

I can't wait till Christmas! I'll come the next weekend AFTER the next weekend! Lots and lots and lots and LOTS of Love,

Dan

Nine Unexpected Odd Facts

1. Dopey Dan writes good letters.

2. Cigarettes look cool but feel hot.

3. Cheese smells foul but tastes good. PONG

4. Eggs looks sweet when he's fast asleep.

5. One titchy little chocolate bar contains 350 calories. → CHOC

6. The hippest deadliest rock stars have the mumsiest of mums.

7. An outfit that looks truly great in the changing room becomes hideous the moment you get it home.

8. Likewise, new shoes that fit perfectly in the shop rub and pinch the moment you step into the street. OUGH!

9. A boy can be mega-brainy but very s-l-o-w to catch on.

Seventh Heaven

'Of course Dan can come and stay the weekend after next,' says Anna. 'Oh, Eggs! Watch your juice. You're spilling it *all*.'

'No! You weren't *listening*,' I say. 'I don't *want* him to come.'

'I thought you just said you did,' says Anna, stripping Eggs stark naked and stuffing his pyjamas straight into the washing machine.

'I'm all bare. Look at my willy, Ellie,' says Eggs, practically waving it at me.

'Yuck. Can't you stuff him in the washing machine too, Anna?' I say.

She's on her knees, sorting through the dirty clothes basket, juggling little balls of socks.

'You just wish you had a willy too,' says Eggs.

'Attaboy, Eggs,' says Dad, finishing his coffee.

'You've got these women sussed out. Right, I'm off.'

'Why are you going so early?' says Anna. 'Can't you wait and take Eggs to school?'

'No, there's someone I've got to catch,' says Dad, scooping up Eggs with one arm and giving him a kiss.

'Who?' says Anna, her fists clenching.

'Oh, for God's sake. Jim Dean, the graphics guy. Anna, don't start.'

'It's not me that starts things, it's you,' says Anna. 'OK OK, you go to work. Just make sure you come home on time. I'm not going to miss my Italian class again.'

'You and that wretched evening class. You go on about it as if it's the most important thing in your life,' says Dad as Eggs wriggles free.

'What else have I got in my life?' Anna says bitterly. She holds out an armful of smelly socks. 'My life is so full and so rich and so exciting. Here I am, sorting your dirty socks. Wow, I can barely contain my excitement. Why can't you smooth them out straight for a start? Why should I have to unravel them all? Why can't you put them in the machine? You keep kidding yourself you're still a young man. So why don't you act like a *new man* and do your share of the chores?'

'Why can't you act like the young woman you are instead of a bitter old nag?' says Dad, and he walks out.

Anna bursts into tears as the front door slams.

'Mum?' says Eggs. 'Have you hurt yourself?'

'Get *washed*, Eggs. And put your clothes on,' I say, steering him towards the door.

'Mummy do it,' says Eggs.

'Don't be such a baby. Mum's tired. Now off you go. I'll take you to school.'

'I don't want *you* to take me to school. Dad takes me.'

'Listen, Squirt. You wash. You get dressed. You do as I say. And then I *might* tell you the Egg story on the way to school.'

'Oh, wow. Right. OK,' says Eggs, whizzing off. He pauses at the door. 'Mum? Isn't it getting better?'

'Yes. Mmm. I'm fine now,' says Anna, sniffing. 'Go on, go and get washed, lickety spit.'

Eggs rushes off, mumbling 'Lick and spit, lick and spit, lick and spit.'

'Thanks, Ellie,' says Anna.

'Anna. You and Dad . . .?'

'Oh. It's — it's just a bad patch.'

'Anna . . .' I stand still in the quiet kitchen. 'Anna, there isn't anyone else, is there?'

Anna's head jerks. 'Someone else?' she says. She's staring at me, her face very white. 'Why? What makes you say that? What do you know? Ellie?'

'I don't know anything. I just wondered . . . Well, Dad can be a right pain at times, and if you've met someone else at your Italian class, well, it's scary because it's horrid with you and Dad arguing like this, but I do understand. I know I always used to take Dad's side but now I'm older — well, I wouldn't *blame* you if you had an affair, Anna.'

Anna is staring as if she can hardly believe what I'm saying. Then she shakes her head, half laughing, though she's still got tears in her eyes. '*I'm* not having an affair, you chump,' she says.

'Then . . .?' I suddenly *realize*. 'Is *Dad*?'

'I don't know. He says he isn't. I say he is. Sometimes I think he's telling the truth and I'm just paranoid. Other times I'm sure he's lying,' says Anna, hurling the socks into the machine along with all his other stuff.

'Who do you think it is?'

'Some girl in his Art class. I don't know her name but I saw her hanging on his arm in the town. Very young, very pretty, with a lot of blond hair.'

'Well, couldn't they just have been walking along together?'

'Maybe. But I saw the way he was looking at her. The way he used to look at me.'

'Oh, Anna.' I hover helplessly.

'I'm sorry,' says Anna, shutting the door of the washing machine and getting to her feet. 'I shouldn't have said anything. It's probably all my imagination anyway. It's just when I get started I can't stop. It's just . . . I love him so.'

That's the weirdest bit. I think about it as I take Eggs to school. I'm busy making up this daft serial story he likes about the Eggstremely Ovoid Eggles – there's Mama Eggle, Papa Eggle, Grandma and Grampy Eggle, and hundreds of eggy little Eggles, Edward, Edwina, Edith, Enid, Ethelred, Ethan, Evangeline . . . and they all sleep in an Eggidorm which has a big bed with oval segments for the eggles to snuggle in and then when they get up in the morning they wobble to a hole in the floor and whizz down this slide to get their breakfast in the kitchen down below. They only ever eat cornflakes – they hate and detest cooked breakfast. And then there are their cousins the Chockies who only visit at Easter and they hate hot weather . . .

I go on and on and it gets sillier and sillier, but Eggs adores it. After a while my mouth takes over and tells the story while my mind thinks about Anna and Dad. How can she still love him like that? I suppose *I* love him, but he's my dad. I couldn't *stick* him as my partner, especially if he started playing around. Anna must have got it wrong. Why on earth would any pretty young student fall for my dad? And yet Anna did exactly that. I can't understand it. Dad isn't even good looking as old guys go. Why don't they want someone young and gorgeous like . . .

Oh, God, it's him! My Dan! The dream one, with the blond hair and the brown eyes. I haven't seen him for ages. I gave up on him and started getting the bus every day. But now he's walking towards me, getting nearer. I think he's looking at me, he *is*! Oh, what shall I do? I look away. Oh, please don't let me blush. I'm getting hot, he's getting nearer still—

'Ellie? Ellie, what's up? Go on with the Eggle story!' Eggs demands, tugging at my arm as if it's a water pump.

'In a minute,' I mutter.

'*Now!*' Eggs demands. 'You promised.'

He's right in front of me. I look up and he's smiling, he's really smiling. Then he shakes his head at Eggs. 'Little brothers!' he says to me.

I nod, dumbstruck.

'See you,' he says, and he walks on.

'See you,' I whisper, dazed.

'Ellie? Who's that man?' Eggs demands.

'Shh!' I hiss. 'I don't know.'

'Why have you gone red?'

'Oh, God, have I?'

'Ever so. Go on with the Eggles story, *please*.'

I blurt out a few dumb Eggle incidents, inventing a new egg who is made of solid gold, so gleaming yellow that he dazzles everyone.

I deliver Eggs to his primary school and dawdle off in the general direction of my school. I'm going to be late, of course, but I can't possibly dash. I need to savour this moment. He said 'See you.' He really did. I didn't make him up. He was there, he spoke to me, and he said 'See you.' Which means, See you again! Or even, I *want* to see you again!

Oh, I want to see *you* again, so much.

All my problems with the insistence of the real Dan seem unimportant. I can't even worry too much about Dad and Anna now. This is one of the most magical moments of my life. I feel like . . . Juliet.

I wish I dared bunk off school and drift around all day hanging on to this feeling. But I trudge there eventually and get seriously told off for my pains. Nadine is still being all cold and huffy and when we do PE we see another love-bite, lower down this time. Magda and I can't help boggling at it as Nadine hurriedly pulls on her games shirt.

'What are you staring at?' she says.

'Nadine! Isn't it flipping *obvious*?' says Magda. 'Can't you get Liam to eat a decent meal before he goes out with you? He seems to want to slurp great gobbets out of you all the time.'

'Just mind your own business, OK?' says Nadine.

Magda shrugs and saunters out of the changing rooms. I hang back. Nadine knows I'm still here but she bends down, fussing with her shoes. Her hair swings forward and I see the startlingly white scalp at her parting. I remember when we used to play hairdressers and how I loved to brush Nadine's long soft rustling hair, so different from my own mass of wire wool.

'Naddie-Baddie,' I say softly. I haven't called her that since we were in the infants.

She looks up and she's suddenly herself again. 'Ellie-Smellie,' she says.

'Oh, Nad. Make friends, eh?'

'I didn't ever *break* friends.'

'Yes, but you've been all cold and narky.'

'Well, you started it, gabbing to Magda.'

'I know, I'm sorry. I could have bitten my tongue off for telling her. Look.' I stick my tongue out and mime biting it. I'm a little too enthusiastic with my demonstration and my teeth sink in before I can stop them. '*Ouch!*'

'Oh, Ellie, you are a nutcase.' Nadine gives me a quick hug. 'We're friends, OK?'

'I'm so glad. I can't stand *not* being friends with

108

you,' I say, sucking my tongue. 'Are you going to be friends with Magda too?'

'Well, only if she stops giving me grief about Liam. She's just jealous anyway, because he's so dishy, a hundred times better than that Greg of hers.'

'Cheek!' says Magda, who's come running back to see what's happened to me. Then she laughs. 'But certainly partly true. Greg isn't a patch on Liam when it comes to looks. When I first saw your Liam I *was* dead jealous, I admit it. But now . . . Oh, Nadine, can't you see, he's just using you.'

'No, he's not. He really cares about me. He can barely leave me alone when we're together,' Nadine says.

'Yes, but that's just sex, Nadine. That's all he wants. He doesn't even take you out properly. Just gets you to go off on all these walks.'

'He does *so* take me out. We're going to Seventh Heaven on Saturday night,' says Nadine. 'He's got these freebee tickets from a mate.'

'Wow! Seventh Heaven!' I say. It's the newest and baddest and best club. Everyone's desperate to go there. None of our lot has made it yet.

'But what about my birthday?' says Magda. 'I thought you guys were coming round to my place, right? And we would go out all girls together?'

'Oh, God,' says Nadine. 'I forgot, Magda! And these tickets, they're just for Saturday night. Oh, what am I going to do?'

'It's OK,' says Magda. 'You go. Who'd want to pass up a chance to go to Seventh Heaven? Hey! Ellie, how about if you and me go too? I'll get my dad to cough up the cash. Don't worry, Nadine, we won't cramp your style. We'll keep well away from you and Dracula.'

'Dracula indeed!' says Nadine, but she laughs.

It's OK at last. We're all three friends again. And we're going to Seventh Heaven!

I wonder if the blond dreamboat Dan ever goes clubbing???

Nadine is telling her parents she's spending Saturday with Magda. I really *am* – but of course I'm not telling Dad and Anna we're planning to go to Seventh Heaven. My dad loves to act laid back but I know he'd never let me go there in a million years because there's been all this stuff in the local papers for weeks about the fights at four in the morning and girls being rushed to hospital with drug overdoses and all this other seriously heavy stuff. I just tell them Magda's having this little party and I'll sleep over at her place and come home some time on Sunday.

'What are you going to wear to this party?' Dad says. 'Not that T-shirty thing again?'

He's home half an hour *early*, so Anna's all set for her evening class. Dad's trying to act as if the row this morning didn't happen.

'Maybe it's time you had some new clothes, Ellie. Here.' He hands me twenty quid. Then realizes it's not enough. He fumbles in his wallet. 'I haven't got enough cash. Look, why don't you go shopping with Anna, use the credit card?' He looks at Anna. '*Both* of you buy yourself something new, eh?'

Anna looks tense. I'm scared she's going to

110

start another row, start on about guilt money or something – and then *I* won't get my outfit after all. But then she shrugs. 'OK. Sure. So, Ellie – we'll go late-night shopping tomorrow.'

'Can you get home early again and look after Eggs, Dad?' I say. 'He's such a pain to take shopping.'

There. I've fixed Dad now. He can't stay out late and play around. Anna gives me a little nod of acknowledgement.

It turns out that we have fun shopping together. It's almost as if Anna is Magda or Nadine. We wander round Jigsaw and Warehouse and River Island and Miss Selfridge and Anna tries on all this mad stuff and when I see her slinking round the changing room showing off her navel in this really raunchy gear I just fall about laughing and she gets the giggles too and it's like we're two girls together. I dare squeeze into some of the sexier stuff too but it's a BIG mistake. I am the mistake. I am big. Well. F–A–T.

'You're *not* fat, Ellie. For God's sake, you're just perfectly normal size,' Anna insists, although she's Ms Stick Insect herself so she's OK. I'm Ms Big Bumblebee – with the emphasis on the Bum.

'What am I going to *wear*?' I say, after I've tried on 101 outfits and discarded them all. 'I want something hip and cool and now – and yet I look positively indecent in all this stuff.'

'You're just a bit curvy for current fashion,' says Anna. 'You don't want these tacky tops or skimpy little skirts.'

111

'So what else am I going to wear? A black plastic rubbish bag?'

'We'll find you the perfect outfit, Ellie, I promise,' says Anna.

And she does! There's this long tight stretchy skirt that I'm scared might be a bit frumpy, but there's a sexy slit up the back – and then she finds a satin shirt to go over the top and I try it on and it's like – wow! – I'm not me any more. I don't look like some stupid podgy little kid. I look much older. Fifteen. Maybe even sixteen.

'Oh, Anna, it's great!' I say. 'But the two together are going to be ever so pricey.'

'So what?' says Anna. 'Let's go mad.'

She buys a little short bright skirt for herself that is *so* different from her usual check-shirt-and-jeans young–mum style. Anna doesn't look older. She looks much much younger.

'Let's buy some tarty shoes too,' she says.

We strut around in these silly heels, both of us staggering. Then we go for identical black suede shoes with little buckles.

'You have them, Ellie, it's OK,' says Anna.

'No, it's not fair. You saw them first. You have them, Anna.'

'You two are very sweet to each other for sisters,' says the assistant, laughing at us.

'We're not sisters,' says Anna. 'Though it feels like we are sometimes.'

'We're . . . friends,' I says, and it's true. For the moment, anyway.

We both get a pair of black buckled shoes and we

112

dance down the road in them, though we've both got blisters by the time we get home.

Anna's being so sweet I feel bad about telling her lies but I know the moment I mentioned Seventh Heaven she'd morph into strict stepmother mode and say No Way.

So off I go to Magda's on Saturday and we have a fun time with her family. You should see the birthday presents they gave her! It's not as if they're rolling in money either. She gets a VCR for her bedroom and a satin blouse a bit like mine but much more clingy and a huge cuddly bunny and a lacy nightie and a big box of chocs and posh lipstick and nail varnish and lots of CDs and scent and a necklace and a great big basket of smelly stuff.

Nadine sends her a Forever Friends card to show she really wants to make up, with a pair of ultra-sexy black knickers inside. I give Magda a cartoon card I drew myself, with Magda up on a pedestal being worshipped by all these different males, not just Greg and his mates and poor sappy Adam, but people like Mr Lanes the History teacher who is quite dishy in a mature sort of way, and I add all her favourite film stars and rock stars too. It sounds like showing off, but she really loves that card – and my present too. That's home-made as well. Anna helped me make it last night. Magda's always liked the Cookie Monster in *Sesame Street* so I baked her a whole batch of different cookies, chocolate and raisin and cherry, and then when they were cool I put them in a special tin. It's airtight so the cookies can keep, but as we spend most of Saturday afternoon in Magda's room mucking around and watching videos we keep stuffing cookies one after the other, so there aren't many actually left now.

It's a good job my new skirt has an elasticated waistband because Magda's mum gets together this incredible birthday cake and crème brûlée and tiramisú and banoffi pie – *and* all the poached salmon and quiche and chicken and little-sausage-on-stick stuff.

'We'd better watch what we drink at Seventh Heaven or there's going to be a serious chucking-up situation!' Magda whispers.

I'm starting to feel a bit sick actually when we set out. Not because of all the food. Because suddenly Seventh Heaven is the very last place I want to go to. You have to queue up to get in and this awful bouncer guy at the door eyes you up and down and if he thinks you're too young or too wet or too boring he won't let you in.

I don't want to go – but it would still be terrible to be turned away!

'Come on, Ellie! What are you hanging back for?' Magda asks.

'My shoes hurt,' I say – which is true. And the slit in my skirt isn't that big, so my knees are a bit hobbled. 'Magda . . . what if we don't get in?'

'We will. You leave it to me,' says Magda.

'We don't know anyone that goes there.'

'So? We'll be part of this great new crowd,' says Magda. 'And anyway, we know Nadine, don't we?'

It's seriously weird when we get there and join the queue. There are some very tall glam girls with

114

very tarty clothes and lots of make-up who make me feel very small and mousy.

'Clock all those trannies!' says Magda, giving me a nudge.

I blink and take another look. Magda's right, they're boys under all the blusher. And there are ordinary gay guys too, in tight T-shirts and fantastic tight leather trousers, showing off their muscle tone. There are girls too, giggling together, with cropped hair and nose studs.

'I think it's a gay night,' I hiss. 'Oh, Magda, maybe we're going to look stupid if we try to get in tonight.'

'Relax, babe. It's *everybody's* night,' says Magda, nodding at a crowd of guys further up the queue. 'Wow, they look pretty tasty. Now they're not gay, I'm sure of it. And look, there are loads of straight couples too. Can you see Nadine and Dracula?'

I can't see them at all. I just see lots and lots of cool clubby chic people and I feel smaller and sadder every second. We're working our way up the queue now and I'm so scared the guy will yell 'You must be joking, you don't belong here, you silly little schoolgirl,' and then I'll literally shrivel up in my suede shoes and die here and now.

But Magda winks at him saucily and he grins at her and nods us both in, just like that. I can't believe it!

It's so great, seeing inside Seventh Heaven. It's midnight-blue with luminous stars and incredible strobes and the music is so loud and the smoky-cloud stuff pumping all over the place is so strange that I stop being me, Ellie, I'm this new cool clubber and I'm here to have fun. Magda and I have a quick tour round to see if we can spot Nadine but she's not here yet. Magda takes me by the wrist and we get onto the dance floor. I'm not too bad at dancing but I generally worry in case anyone's looking at me and noticing my fat bum but now I just get into the rhythm and leap around like part of the crowd. I *am* the crowd. We're *all* the crowd and it's truly fantastic.

Only we get tired eventually and go to get a drink. Magda orders two vodka and cranberry juices at the bar, but the barman tells her to dream on. So we have the juice without the vodka. It's more refreshing that way.

Then this older guy comes up and starts hitting on Magda, leaning over and whispering in her ear. My heart starts hammering, because what am I going to do if she gets off with someone? – but then Magda shakes her head and he goes away.

'What was he saying?' I ask.

'Oh, he was pushing E and whizz and all that junk,' says Magda.

'*Really?*' I say, staring after this real live drug-pusher.

'It's OK. I made it plain we're not into drugs.'

There are lots of other kids who obviously *are*. As it gets later lots start crashing about, their eyes huge and staring. A girl near us suddenly sits on the floor and starts weeping.

I stare at her, wondering if she's all right. Suddenly Seventh Heaven doesn't seem quite such a glittery place after all. I still can't see Nadine anywhere. Maybe she isn't going to turn up.

Magda and I dance again, and I have to take my shoes off, but I don't dare put them down in case they get kicked away so I dangle them by their straps, which is a bit awkward. I'm starting to get ever so tired. I think Magda is too.

Then way off at the other side of the club, right at the back, I think I see this blond head. My dream guy! Well, maybe not, I can't see properly. Heaps of guys have that amazing fair hair, though I think it really *could* be him, only now there's a whole load of other kids in front of him.

'Let's go over the other side for a bit,' I suggest, trying to sound dead casual, though I have to yell in Magda's ear before she can hear me above the music.

We're edging our way over when we spot Nadine at last. She's dancing wildly, her dark hair flying, her eyes very big, very black, very staring.

'What the hell is she on?' says Magda.

Liam is with her. It's horrible the way he's leering at her.

'Hey, Nadine!' Magda yells, charging over to her. 'You look ever so hot. I think you maybe need a drink. Come to the ladies' room, eh?'

Liam tells Magda to get lost. Magda takes no notice. '*Nadine.* Come on.' Magda takes hold of one arm, I take the other, and we pull her away.

I glance back once but I can't see any blond head now. Maybe I was mistaken anyway.

Nadine is all sweaty and stares at us blearily, practically out of it.

'What has that pig got you to take, eh?' Magda says fiercely. 'You'd better have a drink of water. Several. You're dehydrated. Only not *too* much,' she says, as Nadine bends over the washbasin in the ladies' and starts slurping straight from the tap. 'Honestly! You're like a baby. It's a good job Ellie and I are here to keep an eye on you.'

Magda finds a paper cup and we give Nadine a couple of drinks. Then she staggers off to the loo.

A whole little gang of girls come into the ladies'.

'It's OK, we're not in the queue, we're just waiting for our friend,' Magda tells them.

'She's not the dark-haired girl with that Liam, is she?' says one of the girls.

'So?' says Magda.

'Well, she wants to keep clear of him. He used to hang round this girl at our school, really young, just in Year Eight, or maybe she'd just started Year Nine.'

Magda and I keep stum.

'He has this thing about really young girls. He says if you go with virgins you don't have to bother about safe sex because you can't catch anything off them.'

'*What?*' I say.

'I don't *believe* it!' says Magda.

'It's true. He's done it with lots of girls, but he gives them the elbow the minute they start to put out. This girl at our school, she got pregnant from this one time, but he just told her to get lost, he didn't want to know. He said she was a slag anyway, saying if she'd do it with him then she'd do it with anyone.'

118

Magda and I stare at each other, horrified. Then we look at the cubicle where Nadine is. Surely she must have heard? She stays in there until all the other girls have gone. After a few minutes we hear her crying.

'Come out, Naddie,' I whisper.

'Yes, come on, babe, it's just us,' says Magda.

Nadine comes out, tears streaming down her face. She heard all right.

'We're going to go home,' says Magda, putting her arm round her. 'We'll sneak out the back, leave him standing there. I've got the cab fare. You come back to my place and sleep over with Ellie and me.'

So that's just what we do. And when I wake up at dawn and hear Nadine sobbing in the spare bed I slip over and get in beside her and cuddle her close.

Nine Favourites

1. FAVOURITE BOY: Dream Dan.

2. FAVOURITE GIRL: Nadine and Magda – can't choose between them.

3. FAVOURITE CLUB: Seventh Heaven. OK, it's the only club I've ever been in, but it's definitely the best.

4. FAVOURITE MEAL: pizza with extra toppings of everything, especially pineapple.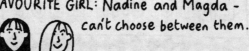

5. FAVOURITE SNACK: Magnum ice-cream.

6. FAVOURITE ANIMAL: elephant. Girl elephants stay with their mothers all their lives - true fact.

7. FAVOURITE COLOUR: purple.

8. FAVOURITE FLOWER: pansy.

9. FAVOURITE TV PROGRAMME:

The X-Files   Friends   Sesame Street

Eight till Late

Dear Dan,

I'm ever so sorry but you really CAN'T come and stay at my home. I did ask, but Anna my stepmother won't allow it. I don't think you realized this on holiday but she's really really strict and right at the moment she's dead annoyed with me because she found out that I went to this amazing club with a serious reputation so now I'm grounded for the rest of the TERM and she says I can't have anyone at all to stay, so I'm afraid it really will be Christmas at the cottages before we see each other again. I do hope you understand and don't feel too mad at me.

L. Ellie   x

My tongue is black all over. It's a wonder it hasn't cracked at the roots and crumbled into cinders in my mouth.

I feel so mean saying all that stuff about Anna. She's been really super to me. And she's never said anything about the night of Magda's party. I came home from Magda's as good as gold on Sunday and said we'd just had this super birthday meal that had lasted practically all evening, but when I kicked off my killer shoes Anna saw my tights were all holes because I'd been dancing so much. She's been an absolute sport and it's especially unfair for me to say she won't let anyone come and stay because next weekend she's letting Magda and Nadine stay over Friday night.

We're all going to Stacy's birthday party. It's going to be great if everyone starts celebrating their birthdays in style – we'll be raving right through the year! Not that Stacy's party is going to be a *rave*. We wondered why on earth she'd asked us to her party because she's not our particular friend, we hardly know her, but it turns out she's asked the entire form, and a lot of girls in Year Nine in the other forms too.

'My mum and dad are hiring the hall at the community centre and there's going to be a disco and a finger buffet and we've got an extension so it's going to be eight till late,' Stacy burbles.

'Wow!' says Magda, but Stacy doesn't twig she's being sarcastic and just grins gratefully.

'Yeah, isn't it fabulous? Well, see you there, you three.'

'We're really looking forward to it . . . *not*,' says Magda, the minute Stacy's back is turned.

'Shut up, she'll hear,' I say. I always feel much more worried about damply enthusiastic girls like Stacy who are so terribly uncool. If I didn't hang around with Magda and Nadine and try really hard to be hip I could so easily be one myself.

But Magda can be caring too. She's looking at Nadine, who hasn't said a word. She's barely spoken since the Seventh Heaven night when she walked out on Liam. She just drifts round after us like this pale little ghost. The purple marks are fading on her neck but it's going to take her much longer to get him to fade from her mind.

'Oh, I don't know, Stacy's party could be a laugh, I suppose,' says Magda. 'We could stick together, us three, and have a bit of a bop. I quite fancy a girls' night out. OK?'

'OK!' I say. 'Right, Nadine?'

I have to nudge her twice before she nods.

But it turns out it isn't going to be a girls' night out at all.

'You can all bring a boy,' Stacy announces. 'My boyfriend Paul is coming. This is going to be a *proper* party.'

'I like *im*proper parties,' says Magda.

'I can't come then,' says Nadine. 'I haven't got a boy. Not any more.'

'Oh, don't go all droopy again, babes, I can't bear it,' says Magda. 'Of course you're coming.'

'Yeah, with me. I haven't got a boy to bring

either, have I?' I say. 'Seeing as my Dan is stuck up in Manchester.'

'I can always ask Greg to bring along two of his mates,' says Magda.

'No way! Not again!' I say very firmly indeed.

It turns out *Greg* won't agree to go to Stacy's party. Magda can't believe it.

'The *nerve* of it! He says he won't go to a stupid Year Nine baby birthday party because his mates would give him stick about it if they found out – after he made *me* go to that night of Ultimate Embarrassment at that nerdy Adam's place! I told him where to get off. Or words to that effect.' Magda grins. 'So now I haven't got a boy either, Nadine. We're a right pathetic trio. One totally absent boyfriend, and two exes.'

'Well, we'll go to Stacy's party just the three of us, like we planned originally. Let's make it a real girls' night out,' I say. 'You two come back to my place and sleep over afterwards, yeah?'

Magda agrees enthusiastically. Nadine doesn't look as if she agrees at all, but she can't summon up the energy to argue.

'I am seriously worried about Nadine,' Magda whispers to me in class. 'Ellie . . . how far did that Liam get with her?'

'I'm not sure. I know he made her do all sorts of stuff, but I'm not sure about actual sex.'

'You don't think . . .? She couldn't be pregnant, could she?'

'Oh, Magda!'

'She looks so pale.'

'Well, she's always pale.'

'Yes, but now she looks like *death*. And she's so droopy.'

'That's because she's missing Liam.'

'How *can* she now she knows the truth about that creep?'

'Maybe she's missing him even so.'

'*What?* Look, I don't get all this moping-around lark. I've just given up Greg and yet I'm not an old droopy-drawers.'

'Yes, but you were never really that gone on Greg, were you?'

'How do you know Greg wasn't the love of my life, the passion of my girlhood, the flame of my bosom, the fire of my loins—?' We are both shrieking with laughter by this time.

Nadine stares over at us but she doesn't even ask what we're laughing at. I look at her tense white face and the dark circles under her eyes. I start to get scared. Could Magda really be right? What if Liam has got Nadine pregnant, just like that other girl?

I know there isn't any point asking her outright, not at school. I'll have to talk to her privately, without Magda.

So after tea this evening I tell Anna I need to borrow a textbook for homework off Nadine. Anna's in a bit of a flap herself because Dad's late home again.

'He'll be in a meeting. Or helping some student with a project,' I say. 'Don't worry, Anna. I'm sure he's not . . . He'll be in any minute, you'll see.'

126

I feel mean leaving her but I have to go round to Nadine's. Nadine's mum asks me how I am and her dad calls me Curlynob as always, but there's something guarded about their welcome.

Natasha is her usual prancy poisonous self: 'Hi, Ellie! Look, do you like my new knickers? They've got frills, see?'

I can't help seeing as she's got her dress hoiked up to the waist. Why are all little kids such exhibitionists? If we carried on like that we'd get locked up — and yet *we're* the ones who're meant to be sex mad.

'Natasha, darling!' says her mum fondly.

'Where's your brother Eggs then, Ellie? Why didn't you bring him round to play with me? I like Eggs,' Natasha gushes, making her eyebrows waggle.

'You little saucepot,' says her dad, pretending to smack her frilly bottom.

Nadine says nothing at all through all this. She stays hunched on the sofa, barely looking at me.

'Nadine! Aren't you going to offer Ellie a drink of Coke or a juice or anything?' her mum hisses.

'It's OK, thanks. I've only just had my tea. I've really just popped over to borrow that History book for homework, Nadine,' I say awkwardly.

Nadine stares at me, as we don't even have History homework this week.

'Let's go up to your bedroom,' I say.

Nadine gets to her feet like it's a huge great effort.

'For Heaven's sake, buck yourself up, Nadine,' says her mum. Then she looks at me. 'I'm sorry, Ellie, but I'm really going to have to stop Nadine going out with you and Magda so much. I think you girls must stay awake half the night when you're sleeping over at each other's houses. Nadine's been like a limp rag just recently and it's really not good enough. Just look at the state of her!'

'Yes, I know, I'm sorry,' I mumble.

When we're out in the hall Nadine raises her eyebrows apologetically for using me as an alibi. I follow her upstairs. The midnight tone of her black walls and gentle spiral of her hanging crystals make her room a soothing bolthole from the aggressive rose wallpaper and pink Axminster on the landing.

Nadine flops down on her bed. I sit beside her, fingering her black quilt. She's sewn it with silver stars.

'Nadine?' I delicately trace the star shapes with my finger, trying to get up the courage to come out with it.

'What?'

'Naddie, look, I wanted to see you, just you and me. To ask . . . to ask how you are.'

'You can see how I am,' says Nadine, turning on her side.

'Well. I know you're feeling pretty fed up.'

'That's the understatement of the century.'

'I'm sorry. I'm making a muck of this. It's just — oh, Nadine, I can't stand to see you like this. We thought, Magda and me, that maybe . . . maybe . . ?'

'Maybe what? I wish you and Magda would quit discussing me. Aren't you both happy now?' Nadine says bitterly. 'You can both say I told you so because

128

you've been right all along about Liam and I've made an utter fool of myself.'

'Oh, Nad, we don't think that. It's just you said you did all this stuff with Liam and I couldn't help wondering – well, if you went the whole way with him and if you could possibly . . .' I lower my head so I'm whispering right into her ear. '. . . possibly be pregnant.'

Nadine lies still for a moment. I hold my breath. Then she looks up. Her eyelashes are spiky with tears. 'No,' she says. 'No, I didn't. And no, I'm not. I wanted to, just to show Liam how much I love him, but whenever he tried to I was suddenly too scared and I went so tense we couldn't. So he said I was frigid.'

'Oh, for God's sake! *Nadine!* That's the oldest and dirtiest trick in the book.'

'I know. But I just wanted to please him. So on Saturday he gave me this stuff to relax me. We were going to go on to his mate's place afterwards, where we could have a proper bed, because Liam thought it was maybe doing it out in the open that was bugging me. But then you and Magda came over. And then I heard those girls . . .'

'Well, I know it must be awful for you, but at least you know what he's really like now.'

'But – but I got to thinking – I mean, what if those girls were talking about some other Liam?'

'You have to be joking. They saw him. *Your* one.'

'Or maybe they were making it all up because they were jealous because they wanted him themselves.'

'Nadine, you can't believe this crap!'

'Well, that's what I started telling myself. So I thought I ought to see Liam just to find out.'

'No!'

'And so yesterday after school I went looking for him, and when I found him with a whole crowd outside the video shop he wouldn't even speak to me properly. He just said he never wanted to see me again after walking out on him like that in Seventh Heaven. He said I was a tight bitch, so cold that going with me would be like bonking a bag of Bird's Eye frozen peas, and all his mates laughed, and this girl started hanging on his arm and cuddling up to him and sneering at me . . .'

'Oh, Naddie, Naddie!' I put my arms round her and held her tight.

'Don't tell Magda, will you?'

'I swear I won't.'

'I feel so stupid. And ashamed. He was so awful to me, and yet — yet I still feel I *love* him. Do you think I'm completely nuts, Ellie?'

'No, of course not. It's *him* who's the really vicious nutter.'

'I wish it wasn't all such a mess. If only I had someone who really loved me back. Someone romantic. Something like your Dan, writing to you all the time.'

I take a deep breath. 'Nadine. About Dan . . .'

Nadine looks up at me. 'What about him?'

I open my mouth. The words are there, buzzing in my brain. I just have to trigger my tongue into action. Say it, Ellie. SAY IT!

'I made him up.'

I say it so quickly it comes out as one weird word: *Imadimup*.

Nadine blinks, not quite getting it at first. Then – 'Ellie! You made him *up*?'

'Well, sort of. There was this boy on holiday, but he wasn't . . . and then there was this *gorgeous* guy, and he *did* talk to me once, but he's not called Dan, the other one is.'

'What are you *on* about?'

'I don't know. It's all a muddle. The thing is, my Dan isn't mine and he's not even called Dan. So if there's anyone who's completely nuts it's me, saying all this stupid stuff about a boyfriend when I've never ever had one, not a proper one, anyway.'

'I just can't get my head round this! I *did* wonder, just at first – but you were so *convincing*. Hey, have you told Magda?'

'No! I couldn't bear it if she knew. She'd have such a laugh at me. You won't tell her, will you, Nad?'

'I promise I won't. Oh, God, Ellie, we're a right pair, aren't we?'

'You're telling me.'

'We're a right pair.'

'You're telling me.'

'We're a . . .'

'You're telling . . .'

We're laughing so much we can hardly speak. It's an age-old routine we used to spout when we were about seven and it wasn't really funny then. But it feels so good to giggle like crazy. We both roll on the bed, helpless – and we're truly back to being Best Ever Friends.

Nadine's still dead depressed about Liam, of course, but she's not in quite such a zombie trance.

I tell Magda there are no worries on the pregnancy front.

'You're sure, Ellie?'

'Positive. They never actually did it.'

'Well, at least that's something. Though it still beats me how Nadine can have been *mad* enough to go with a guy like that.'

'Well, we all do crazy things sometimes, Magda,' I say uncomfortably. 'Let's stop going on about it, eh?'

Magda is happy enough to change the subject because she's found out that Stacy has this older brother Charles who's going to be keeping an eye on things at the party, and apparently he's really quite tasty looking, with blond hair.

'How old?' I ask.

'About eighteen, according to Amna. She's been to Stacy's house for tea.'

Stacy's got big brown eyes.

'Are his eyes brown by any chance?' I say, though I know it's a chance in a million. Well, there aren't a million people who live in our town. Ten thousand? But that's everybody. How many halfway good-looking boys of eighteen are there? The odds are whittling downwards. A thousand to one? Maybe even a hundred to one?

'I don't know about his eyes, Ellie. You'll be

asking me for his inside leg measurement next! Ask Amna. Ask Stacy.'

I'd feel a right fool asking Stacy about her brother's eyes. I decide I'll just have to wait and see for myself. Of course he might not even deign to come to this party. But it's getting quite famous now and all sorts of extra people are going. A whole crowd of Year Tens who go to Stacy's dance class are going to be there, and several of them are going out with Year Eleven boys.

Greg is waiting for Magda after school.

'What do *you* want?' she says, linking in with me and Nadine.

Greg scurries along behind us. 'About this old party on Friday night, Magda,' he puffs. 'Hey, wait a minute. I want to *talk* to you.'

'Well, I don't want to waste my breath on you, Greg, so why don't you just push off?' Magda sings over her shoulder.

'Don't be like that. Look, I've changed my mind. I'll go to the party with you, Magda. OK? That's what you wanted, isn't it?'

Magda sighs. She stops. 'That *was* what I wanted. God knows why. It's certainly *not* what I want now. I'm going to the party with my girlfriends. Right, girls?' Magda smiles at us. We smile back, and the three of us walk on, still linked.

There's a pause.

'Well, see if I care,' Greg yells. He's obviously trying hard to come up with something ultra-crushing. 'You girls. You're just a lot of *lezzies*.'

133

We burst out laughing.

'Poor Greg. He's history,' says Magda. 'I like the sound of this Charles. I just have a feeling. Maybe Stacy's party is going to be a key event in our lives, even though we started off thinking it the naffest non-event of the year. Maybe we'll all have a dream encounter there. Are you listening, Nadine? And maybe you'll meet your dream guy too, Ellie – or are you too involved with Dan to be interested?'

I hesitate. I don't dare look at Nadine. I mumble something about always being interested and then change the subject as quickly as I can.

But as the three of us get ready round at my place to go to Stacy's party on Friday evening I can't help hoping that Magda is right. Maybe Stacy's brother might *just* be my dream Dan. I haven't caught a glimpse of him since he said See you.

'*Please* let me see him tonight,' I say over and over again inside my head as I put on my new shirt and skirt and the killer shoes.

I think I look pretty cool, but when I see Magda I feel depressed. She's wearing a brand-new raunchy red number and she's got this new glossy red lipstick that makes her mouth incredible, a shiny scarlet Cupid's bow.

'Want to borrow my lipstick, Ellie?' she says.

I have a go but my lips are too big and my face too fat. I look like a little girl who's been at the strawberry jam. I sigh and rub it off and start again.

'What about you, Nadine? Want to add a bit of colour to your old chops?' says Magda.

'Colour!' says Nadine, shuddering. She's

powdered herself chalk-white and outlined her eyes with kohl. Her own lipstick is such a dark purple it looks black and she's done her nails to match. She looks pretty stunning in a black skirt and a black lacy top and black pointy boots.

'Nice to see you looking your own deathly vampire self again, Nadine,' I say.

I wonder if the dream Dan might go for Nadine's gothic glamour or Magda's sexy scarlet. It seems very very very unlikely that he'll plump for me instead. Plump being the operative word.

But when we get to Stacy's party her brother Charles doesn't go for any of us.

He's not my dream Dan. Well, I knew it would be *way* too much of a coincidence. He *is* pretty tasty though, in a sort of floppy-haired posey kind of way. Stacy is charging about in a flouncy fancy frock, shrieking and squeaking in batty birthday-girl mode, so it's left to big brother Charles to welcome us three into the party and show us where to leave our jackets and stuff.

'So glad you could come,' he says, smiling, looking at us with big blue eyes. (*Not* as distinctive as brown, but pretty devastating all the same.)

I go all girly and Nadine manages a smile and Magda is in Total Vamp mood, her red mouth wide open as if she's about to gobble him up. But then this other girl comes up to us, also smiling. She's taller, older, even glossier than Magda's lipstick. Charles puts his arm round her. She's his girlfriend.

'Oh, well, never mind. Let's hope there are plenty

of other spare guys,' says Magda, her eyes darting round the already crowded room.

'Honestly! I thought this was our big girls' night out,' I say to Nadine. 'Look at Magda, eyes on stalks, desperate to pull.'

'Oh, well. *I* don't want to meet up with anyone,' says Nadine. 'I don't want to go out with another boy for ages. If *ever*.'

Nadine looks much better but it's obviously going to take months before she's completely over Liam.

But at least she's been out with someone properly, even if he was a right pig. I feel so pathetic that the only boyfriend I've ever had is a pretend one.

It's not such a bad party. The music is OK and there's lots of fancy food and that red wine punch they always give you at teenage parties when they don't want you to get drunk.

We have a glassful each and then we have a dance and then a laugh with some of the girls in our class. I suppose it's a good night out, but I can't help feeling depressed when I see that even Stacy has a reasonably good-looking boyfriend and lots of the other girls are with their boys, and though there *are* a few spare boys none of them so much as glances in my direction.

They do quite a lot of glancing at Magda, of course. And Nadine gets her fair share of attention too. But there's no-one here for me. No-one interested in me. No-one at all.

'Ellie?' Stacy suddenly comes rushing over. 'Ellie, there's this boy, he says he knows you. He wants to come to the party. *Do* you know him?'

She points over to the door. I peer through the blurry lenses of my glasses, wondering if it could possibly somehow be my dream Dan.

It *is* Dan.

Not the dream one.

The *real* Dan . . .

Nine Most Embarrassing Moments

1. Dan turning up at Stacy's party.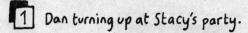

2. Wetting myself up on the stage at primary school.

3. Going swimming in a bikini and the top coming unhooked.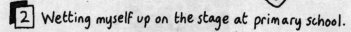

4. Starting my period one night when I was staying over with Nadine, so that I got blood on the bedclothes.

5. Hearing what my voice really sounds like when Magda and I sang during a Karaoke session.

6. Trying on clothes in a changing room full of beautiful girls who only weigh about six stone.

7. Getting a boil on my bum and having to show the doctor.

8. Forgetting my PE shorts to get out of hockey and Mrs Henderson making me play in my school shirt and knickers.

9. Making such a fool of myself whenever I meet Dreamboat Dan.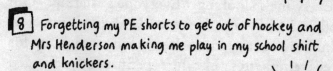

I stare at him. It *can't* be. It *is*.

But how? I told him not to come. So what the hell is he doing here? How did he know where I was?

He hasn't seen me yet. Oh no. He has. He's grinning. Waving. At me.

'What on earth?' says Magda.

'Who *is* he?' says Nadine.

Everyone's looking. Everyone's staring. Oh, God, he looks worse than ever. *His hair!* It's not even a skinhead cut any more. It's sticking straight up for three centimetres, like he's permanently plugged into a live wire. And he's wearing a totally nerdy huge white T-shirt with a silly message and his jeans are showing his ankles and he's wearing ancient Woollies trainers. They squeak as he crosses the

140

polished floor. Squeak, squeak, squeak at every step. Nearer and nearer. And everyone's still staring, whispering, giggling.

'Who *is* this berk?' Magda says, giving me a nudge.

'I don't know,' I mutter madly.

'Hi, Ellie!' Dan shouts above the disco music.

'Well, he knows you!' says Nadine.

'Oh no,' I say, and I turn, desperate, wondering if I can make a run for it.

'Ellie? Hey, wait! It's me, Dan!'

'*Dan?*' says Magda.

'*Dan?*' says Nadine. 'How can it be Dan? You said you made him up.'

'Well this guy looks all too real,' says Magda, giggling. '*He's* your boyfriend, Ellie?'

'No!' I insist, but he's got to me now, trampling past everyone in his awful trainers, a silly grin still ear to ear.

'Hi, Ellie. Surprise!' he says, as he lunges forward.

I'm so terrified he's going to put his arms round me in front of everyone that I step back sharply and spear Stacy with one of my killer heels. She squeals.

Dan's arms are stretched out. They stay empty, clutching at air. The grin fades from his face. He swallows. He doesn't know what to say, what to do. And everyone's still staring. He's going red right to the tips of his ears. They stick out so with his new silly haircut. His glasses are starting to steam up. His eyes look agonized. Oh, poor Dan!

'Hello,' I say weakly. 'Meet my best friends, Magda and Nadine.'

141

They are still staring at him as if he's just arrived from Planet Nightmare.

'This is my friend Dan,' I say.

Magda and Nadine give him a little nod, both struck dumb.

'So . . . what are you *doing* here?' I say.

'I wanted to surprise you. I'd set it all up for this weekend, and even when you said your stepmum wouldn't stand for it I thought I could maybe just turn up and sort of sweet-talk her because I thought she was really nice on holiday and she *is* nice, she said she didn't mind a bit if I stay the weekend, even though it's going to be a bit of a squash with your friends staying too. And your dad gave me a lift here and so . . . here I am.'

'Yes. Well. You've certainly surprised me,' I say.

'Shocked, more like,' says Dan.

'I hope you realize you've just about crippled me, Ellie,' Stacy says, still rubbing her foot.

'I'm sorry.'

'So. Is this your boyfriend?' Stacy says, and her eyes are gleaming.

'No!' I say.

'Yes!' says Dan.

Oh, God. Stacy isn't half enjoying this. So is everyone else. No-one's even dancing now. They're stopped for the cabaret. The comic turn. Ellie and Dan.

'Well, is he or isn't he?' Stacy persists.

'Dan's a boy. And Dan's a friend. That's it,' I say. I look at Dan. 'Come and get a drink, eh?'

We walk over to the drinks table together. I go

tock–tock–tock in my killer shoes. Dan goes squeak-squeak-squeak in his tatty trainers.

'Everyone's staring at us,' Dan says.

'I know.'

'This maybe wasn't such a good idea,' says Dan.

'Well . . .'

'I bet you're wishing I hadn't come. I'm showing you up in front of all your cool mates,' says Dan.

'Don't be silly,' I say – but I don't sound very convincing.

'You'd better kiss me quick,' Dan says.

'*What?*'

'Then I'll unzip my frog-suit and step out this hip handsome prince,' says Dan, running his fingers through the lethal stubble of his hair. He tugs at it ruefully. 'The new hairstyle doesn't help, does it?'

'You said it,' I say. 'Well, what are you going to drink? There's not much selection actually. Coke. Or red wine punch.'

'My favourite tipple,' says Dan. 'I'll grab some sandwiches too, I'm starving. We drove straight down south, no stopping at any motorway caff. I was just so desperate to see you.'

'Oh, Dan.'

'True. I might be the last boy on earth you want as a boyfriend but I'd give anything for you to be my girlfriend. You look fantastic, Ellie.'

'Rubbish.'

'Look, I'm doing my best to be dead romantic. Like Romeo and Juliet. Only if I came to serenade you at night you'd come out on your balcony and tip a bucket of water all over me, right?'

'Probably.'

'I don't know. I'm at a bit of a loss as to how to impress you. Travelling long-distance to see you is a no-no. Sweet-talk turns sour. There's not much point trying to dazzle you with my brawny body.' He flexes his puny arm so that his baggy sleeve flaps.

'Did you say brawny – or scrawny?' I say.

'Cruel! OK OK, Arnie Schwarzenegger can relax for the moment. So – what about my ready wit?'

'Er . . . wit or twit?'

'Ouch. God, you've got a wicked tongue.' He raises his glass and drinks to me. Then shudders. 'What *is* this stuff? It tastes like undiluted Ribena.'

'I think it's the key ingredient.'

'Oh well. I'll have another slug or six to get up some Dutch courage before I dare ask you to dance.'

'Maybe it might be better to put that request on hold,' I say.

I'm proved right. Someone starts playing the naughty version of that old Alice song and everyone starts dancing again.

'Come on, let's give it a go,' says Dan.

Major mistake!

Dan has a whole new dance style all his own. Bouncy-bouncy in his squeaky-squeaky trainers. With head nodding, arms whirling. One arm catches someone on the shoulder, another on the chest.

'Sorry, sorry!' he shouts and moves away from them. Nearer me. He bounces again and lands straight on my killer shoes.

'Oh, God, I'm sorry, Ellie. Have I hurt you?'

'It's OK. I think I'm just crippled for life – but I'll

get used to it. So. Maybe we'd better sit this one out.'

We sit at the side, sipping our drinks, watching the others. Magda and Nadine are dancing together. They glance in our direction rather a lot.

'Your friends are very striking girls,' says Dan.

'I know.'

'Nowhere near as striking as you, though.'

'Come off it!'

'You're supposed to simper sweetly when I pay you compliments.'

'Simper – or whimper?'

'Look, you're the princess I released from the tower, right? You're meant to be in my thrall.'

'In your *what*?'

'Perhaps I'd better perform some other princely feat. Kill a dragon or two. Rescue you from a fate worse than death.'

'I don't think there's a clamouring horde queueing up to ravage me right now,' I say.

As I say it there's a sudden shout, raised voices, stupid laughter, swearing. People stop dancing, turn and stare. There's a whole crowd of guys over by the door. Strangers with real skinhead haircuts and real tattoos and real cans of Tennants in their hands.

Stacy's brother and her boyfriend and some of the other boys are arguing with them, trying to get them to go.

'Nah, we're staying, right? We've come to join the party, have a little drinkie, have a little dance,' says the biggest boy, tipping his can. He looks round, staggering a little, obviously already out of his head. His mates follow him, egging him on.

'So which bird shall I pick, eh? Where's the bleeding birthday girl?'

Stacy bobs behind her boyfriend, her face white.

The skinhead doesn't see her. There's only one girl not up on the dance floor. It's me.

'Hey, what are you sitting down for, darling? Little bit of a wallflower, are you? Come and dance with me,' he says.

I freeze.

'She's with me,' says Dan. His voice is as squeaky as his trainers.

'You what?' says the skinhead. 'Who the hell are you, creep? Now, come on, darling, dancie-dancie. He grabs me by the wrist and pulls me up. 'Woooaa! Up you get.'

'She doesn't want to dance with you,' says Dan.

'Yes she does, don't you, darling?' says the skin-head, hanging on to me. 'You come and have a little dance with me and my mates.'

'Are you deaf or something?' Dan says desperately.

'Dan! It's OK. Don't argue with him,' I hiss, because I'm so scared there might be a fight. They could have knives.

'There! She *wants* to dance, don't you, sweet-heart?' he says, and he puts his arms round me, his horribly beery breath hot on my cheek. 'That's it – let's get cosy, eh?' he says, his hands on my bottom.

'Leave her alone!' Dan shouts, jumping up.

'Shut him up, eh, Sandy,' the skinhead says.

The heaviest of his mates lumbers over to Dan. There's a thud, a squeal, and then Dan is sprawling on the floor.

'Dan!'

'Shut up or you'll get it too,' says the skin. 'Did you pop him one, Sandy?'

'Help!' Dan screams, staggering up. His white T-shirt is stained dark red. 'He's stabbed me! I'm bleeding, look!'

Screams echo right round the room as Dan lurches forward and then sinks to his knees.

'What you done now, Sandy? Quick! Run for it!' the skinhead yells, shoving me aside and taking to his heels. The others follow him. No-one dares stop them.

'Dan!' I say, bending down, clutching him, trying to prop his head on my knees. 'For God's sake, someone dial 999, and get an ambulance!'

'It's OK,' says Dan, trying to sit up. 'I don't need an ambulance.'

'Are you *crazy*? You've been stabbed!'

'No I haven't,' says Dan, grinning. 'Those thugs have gone, haven't they? I thought they might run for it if they thought I was bleeding to death. I don't think that guy even had a knife. He just punched me in the stomach and I fell over.'

'But the blood!'

'Smell it,' says Dan, holding out his sopping T-shirt.

'Yuck!'

'It's the wine punch. I spilled it all over me.'

'Oh, you *idiot*!' But then I think about it. 'Though it *worked*. They did go.'

'That was real quick thinking, pal,' says Charles. 'It could have got really nasty with those louts.'

'Thank you so much, Dan. You've saved my birthday party from being an absolute disaster,' Stacy gushes.

'Yeah, well done, Dan.'

'Great thinking.'

'Really cool.'

'Hear that, Ellie? I'm *cool*,' says Dan.

'You're wet and sticky, I'll say that,' I say, shifting him off my lap. 'Get up then, I don't want wine all over my new skirt.'

'After I've seriously rescued you from a fate worse than death? I'm heartbroken. You were supposed to tell me you love me and beg me not to die,' says Dan, gingerly getting to his feet and rubbing his stomach.

'Dream on, matie,' I say, because I'm not going to say anything else in front of everyone.

I wait till later, when there's just him and me in a corner. Which is much *much* later, because everyone keeps clustering round, wanting to talk to Dan and congratulate him.

'Your head's going to be so swollen you're never going to squeeze out of the door,' I say.

'Just as well I've had my new haircut then,' says Dan.

'You are a nut,' I say, and I rub my hand over the bristles. 'But . . . you're a *brave* nut. You stuck up for me when they were really scary blokes.'

148

'They'll be pretty scared themselves, thinking they've murdered me,' says Dan.

'I hope they've really cleared off, and they're not hanging round outside waiting to get us,' I say. 'Lucky job my dad's coming to collect us in the car.'

'Hey, Ellie. Nadine and I were thinking,' says Magda, coming over. 'We'll go home to my place, right? You won't want us sleeping over with you if you've got Dan.'

'Ooh, am I sleeping with Ellie then?' says Dan, grinning.

'No you are not! I guess you'll be tucked up with my little brother Eggs, which serves you right. No, Magda, Nadine, *do* come back with me, *please*. It'll be fun.'

And weirdly, it *does* turn out to be fun. Dad arrives dead on twelve and when the four of us thank Stacy she's still being ever so gushingly grateful and she gives me a hug and then she gives Dan a hug too.

'Wow,' says Dan. 'This is definitely my night.'

'You certainly look as if you've been celebrating,' says Dad, taking in Dan's dramatically stained T-shirt.

'Dan's the hero of the hour,' says Magda.

'He fought all these skinheads to protect Ellie,' says Nadine.

'Well – not *exactly*,' I say.

'See, Ellie? All your friends appreciate me,' says Dan. 'Come on, Nadine and Magda, I'll squeeze in with you two in the back. Ellie can sit in the front with her dad. Then she'll maybe get all jealous.'

'You wish,' I say.

When we get back home Eggs wakes up even though we try to be quiet and he's ecstatic when he sees Dan. He runs to him and gives him a great hug and a slobbery kiss. When he realizes Dan will be sharing his bed he goes really bananas, leaping up and down until his pyjamas fall down round his ankles.

'Hey, no indecent exposure in front of the ladies,' says Dan, yanking his pyjamas into place and picking him up. 'Come on, little guy, let's go to bed.'

Anna has been great sorting out pillows and cushions and duvets and sleeping bags so we've all got somewhere to sleep.

'I'm sorry about Dan arriving out of the blue,' I whisper.

'It's OK. In fact he was tremendously sweet, arriving with a battered bouquet of flowers and a crushed box of chocs. He practically went down on his knees to me to beg to stay here. Almost as if he felt I was some utterly unreasonable ogress who had to be appeased.'

'I wonder what gave him that idea,' I say guiltily. 'Anyway, thanks Anna.'

'No problem. I like Dan, he's a sweet boy.'

And amazingly Magda and Nadine think he is too. We stay awake for ages, whispering and giggling. I have to tell the entire Dan story right from the beginning, explaining how I embellished the original Dan into this super dishy hunk based on the fair boy I bumped into on the way to school.

It's not really such a big deal telling them, though it maybe helps that we've all drunk several glasses of wine punch. It's dark too, so I can go as red as the wine and they can't see. Magda and Nadine say I'm seriously screwy, but don't act that surprised. Magda gets interested in the dream man.

'*He's* real, isn't he, Ellie? Is he really-really-really ultra-tasty? Maybe I'll walk your way before school to see if I can spot him.'

'Hands off, you! I saw him first!'

'But you've got the real Dan,' says Nadine. She adds wistfully. 'He's obviously nuts about you.'

'He's obviously nuts, full stop,' says Magda. 'What's up with his *hair*, Ellie?'

'I know, I know.'

'I thought old Greg was a bit dodgy, borderline Anorak Nerd – but Dan is Star Geek of all time. Though he *is* sweet, I must admit,' says Magda.

'You can have a good laugh with him,' I admit.

'Yeah, but what about a good snog?' says Magda.

I think of snogging Dan. Magda and Nadine are imagining it too. We all burst out laughing simultaneously, and have to dive under our duvets or we'll wake everyone up.

I don't surface until gone eleven in the morning. Magda and Nadine are still fast asleep. Magda's on her side, both arms wrapped round her pillow, her mouth in a sexy pucker. She is obviously snogging someone in her sleep. Nadine is lying on her tummy, her black hair a cloak across the pillow. I can't see her face at all but I can hear little sucky sounds. I think she's sucking her thumb.

I sit up and smile at my two friends, and then I pad off to the bathroom. I take my time getting washed and dressed because I want to look halfway decent. But when I get downstairs at last there's no sign of Dan.

Anna gives me a mug of coffee. 'Poor Dan. Eggs was wide awake at six o'clock and begging him to get up and play with him.'

'Where are they now? And Dad?'

'They've gone swimming. I don't know how Dan will manage for a costume. Your dad's old trunks will be far too big and yet Eggs's stuff is far too little. Maybe he'll just wear his underpants.'

'Please, Anna! You're conjuring up an all too graphic image,' I say, sipping coffee.

'So I take it you and Dan aren't going to be the romance of the century,' says Anna. 'And if your dad and I wanted to go out tonight, say, and leave you two here in the house, you're not likely to start up any X-rated bouncing on the beds?'

'I solemnly promise that Eggs will be the only one to bounce on the beds,' I say. 'So, you want Dan and me to babysit?'

'Your dad did wonder . . . There's this jazz concert up in town. And we could maybe have a meal out first. But it's a bit of a cheek asking you. You and Dan probably want to go out somewhere.'

'You go. You and Dad. Anna . . . How are things with you two?'

Anna crosses her fingers. Things certainly *seem* OK when she and Dad go off together at six. Anna is wearing her new skirt. Dad seems to appreciate it enormously. He gives her a little pat on the bum when he thinks I'm not watching. Yuck. Dad is a really sexist pig at times. He's offered to take her to an Italian restaurant so she can try out her newly acquired conversational skills on the waiters. This sounds a bit patronizing if you ask me. But Anna seems happy enough. Love is blind.

I am not in love. I see Dan all too clearly. Anna's washed his T-shirt for him so he's clean – but that's about the only positive thing I can say about his appearance. And the chlorine at the swimming pool has increased the scrubbing-brush tendency of his hair.

But so what? He's really quite good fun to hang around with. When he gets back from swimming and Magda and Nadine crawl out of bed at long last the four of us play a crazy game of Scrabble until Eggs tips up the board accidentally-on-purpose because he can't bear not to join in too.

We listen to my CDs for a while and Magda and Nadine are a bit scornful because Dan isn't very hip in his musical tastes. But then we get cracking on some of Dad's seventies stuff and Dan comes into his own. He does a brilliant Freddie Mercury imitation, prancing round the living room until we're all in stitches – and then we get going on ancient strutting Stones stuff, and then right back to Elvis. Dan teaches Eggs to flip a quiff of hair and wiggle his hips. Then the boys say it's our turn so I dig out my Beatles compilation. I sing 'With a Little Help from My Friends' (*with* a little help, etc.) and Nadine does her version of 'Lucy in the Sky with Diamonds' and Magda chooses 'All You Need is Love', and then we all sing 'Hey Jude' over and over and then 'Hello, Goodbye'.

Then Magda and Nadine say goodbye and Dan and I watch Wallace and Gromit videos with Eggs. Eggs badgers me until I make him his own plasticine Wallace and Gromit. Dan tries to make stuff too but his things go all hunched and lumpy so he says they're aliens from outer space. So we all make plasticine aliens. I make my alien very thin with sticky-up short hair and big ears. Dan laughs and Eggs plays with it so enthusiastically that the alien's legs fall off.

'Imagine your legs falling off!' says Dan, and then he keels over onto the sofa, pretending his own have done just that. Eggs squeals and jumps on top of him.

'Come on, Ellie!' Eggs yells.

'Er . . . no, thanks!' I say.

Eggs is still bouncing about, full of beans, when Dad and Anna set off for their night out. Anna's left all sorts of stuff in the fridge for tea and Dad's given us a tenner in case we'd sooner go to a McDonald's.

We decide on the McDonald's. We've got no transport and it's a good half-hour's walk, but maybe it'll help tire Eggs out at long last.

I get just a tiny bit tense wondering if there'll be anyone I know at McDonald's but it's still early and it's mostly families. Dan pretends we're a family too, Ma and Pa and Little Egbert, which makes Eggs chuckle. I hadn't realized you could play daft pretend games with boys. He's really great at it too. Nadine used to be good at imaginary games but she won't do it so much now we're older, and Magda's never gone in for that sort of thing anyway.

I see someone I do know on the way home. Well,

I don't *know* him. Though I've thought about him so much I feel as if I've known him all my life. I stare at him and it's as if the real and the pretend are all mixed up for a moment. Then they separate out, and I'm with the real Dan, and this is the dream Dan, though he's certainly not called Dan and it's even more unlikely that he ever dreams about me.

He's with someone. Not a girl. Another boy, almost as good looking, but dark, with blue eyes. Dream Dan's in black, the dark boy's in white. They look great together. And then I realize something else. They *are* together.

They're chatting and laughing, looking at each other – but just as they're going past the dream Dan sees me. 'Hi there!' he says.

'Hi,' I say, smiling wistfully.

The real Dan stares. 'Do you know him?' he says, when we're past.

'Yeah. Well. Sort of.'

'He's ever so good looking,' says Dan, and *he* sounds wistful now. He peers round at them. 'Is that his boyfriend?'

'It looks like it,' I say, sighing.

'Are you Ellie's boyfriend?' Eggs asks Dan.

'Definitely,' says Dan.

'Not even possibly,' I insist.

Dan *isn't* my boyfriend. OK OK, he's fun. And I have a good time with him. And I can say all sorts of stuff to him. And though he's a hopeless nerd he's also brave. And quick-witted. And imaginative. And it doesn't really matter one hundred per cent if he looks stupid. Anyway, I'm hardly some Pamela

Anderson type pin-up. He's not cool. But maybe the *truly* cool guy doesn't care if he's cool or not. But he's still not my boyfriend because I could never get *romantic* about Dan. Not in a Romeo and Juliet kind of way. I'm not too fond, like Juliet. No true-love passion.

Although . . .

We play Ma and Pa as we bath Eggs and put him to bed (which is a struggle, and takes hours). Then we settle down in front of the telly with Coke and crisps. We chat and crunch companionably. We laugh at something daft on the video and Dan rolls one way on the sofa and I roll the other way, towards him. And guess what? We kiss. My first real kiss. And it's not at all the way I imagined it. I didn't crack up laughing. I like it. Even though it's only Dan.

Maybe *because* it's Dan . . .

Nine Romantic Couples

1. Romeo and Juliet.

2. John Lennon and Yoko Ono.

3. Queen Victoria and Prince Albert.

4. Kermit and Miss Piggy.

5. Julian Clary and Fanny the Wonder Dog.

6. Jane Eyre and Mr Rochester.

7. Elizabeth Bennett and Mr Darcy.

8. Morticia and Gomez Addams.

9. Ellie and Dan ???

GIRLS UNDER PRESSURE

Sequel to *Girls in Love*

Jacqueline Wilson

Hi, I'm Ellie. Ellie-Belly. Ellie-phant. That's what I get called by my annoying little brother, Eggs, and even by my best friends, Magda and Nadine It's because I'm so fat. And I hate it. I'm going on a diet right this minute.

No more strawberry ice cream. No more bacon sandwiches. My step-mother tries to help by saying she'll go on a diet too, but she's skinny already. So is Nadine – so thin she could be a cover girl on a magazine. And Magda's got a perfect figure – she has to fight the boys off (literally, sometimes). They're not being much help, but I'm determined . . .

In this moving and funny sequel to *Girls in Love*, Ellie, Magda and Nadine each try out some drastic changes to their looks but none of it works out quite the way they planned. What should they do? These girls are under pressure . . .

Corgi
0 552 54522 8

GIRLS OUT LATE

Sequel to *Girls in Love* and *Girls Under Pressure*

Jacqueline Wilson

How late can YOU stay out? Nine o'clock. That's when *I* have to be home. Dad thinks it's not SAFE any later. But then the most amazing, magical thing happens. Out with my best friends, Magda and Nadine, I meet a boy. And it's ME he's interested in! ME! Plain, plum Ellie. Not drop-dead gorgeous Magda. Nor super-cool Nadine. ME! But will Russell stay interested in a girl who has to be home by nine . . .?

'Jacqueline Wilson . . . has a cult following among older girls for her wacky, comic series about three best friends' *Financial Times*

'Jacqueline Wilson's terrific books about three chums called, Ellie, Magda and Nadine [are] . . . sharp, funny, easy to read and they cover just abut everything you might want to know about the messy, angst-ridden business of growing up today' *Daily Telegraph*

Doubleday hardback
0 385 40806 4
Corgi
0552 54523 6